HIDDEN CAVE

ARMAND ROSAMILIA

HIDDEN CAVE

WWW.SEVEREDPRESS.COM

ISBN: 978-1-923165-33-5

CHAPTER ONE

Sally Rodriquez was farther from her home in Brooklyn than she'd ever been, and it was frightening and exciting at the same time.

"Don't go too far," her mother yelled from the shore, giving her daughter a wave.

Sally groaned. She was fifteen, nearly a woman, and she didn't need anyone's advice or anyone to look over her. She knew what she was doing.

The ceiling was lost above her in the darkness. The water was cool. She could see nearly to the bottom in places, closer to where the lights were set in the cave.

Son Doong was massive, and she'd heard the guide say it was the biggest cave system in the world. Sally believed it. They'd been inside for hours and hadn't made a real dent in what they'd seen so far.

Her parents had visited Vietnam and the cave systems years ago, before she was born, and before Son Doong had been found. This would be their third trip to Vietnam, where Sally's great grandparents had been born. She didn't think her father had ever met them, but he loved talking about his ties to the country, even though subsequent family members had been born in Spain and then her father in Brooklyn.

On her mother's side it was truly Spanish, either Mexican, Brazilian or from Ecuador. That's what Sally had always been told, anyway. She was Latina. They rarely, if ever, spoke about having any other blood in the family tree.

Except when it came to these trips to Vietnam, Sally supposed. For the past several months it was all they talked about. Plans as to what they'd do when they arrived. Her father had put Son Doong at the top of his list, especially since one of his coworkers had gone last year.

Told them all about the caves, the crystal-clear water and the hidden spots.

Her parents had immediately booked a trip for the three of them. Sally had been very blessed with having parents with money, who were younger and liked to travel.

Every year since Sally could remember they'd visited exotic places: Cayman Islands, Italy, Alaska, Japan, Australia, Norway and Mexico. Lots of big and small cities in the United States as well.

Her friends said she was spoiled, and Sally knew it was true.

Sally swam a few laps back and forth across the surface of the natural pool, marveling at how far it went, lost in darkness.

As soon as her father's coworker had told Sally's father the water looked amazing, but you were forbidden to swim in it, her father knew that's exactly what they'd do.

They hated going to the beach. Too much sun and sand. Too many people on Fire Island and Jones Beach, too. Unless you arrived before first light, you'd never find a spot big enough for your family. Forget trying to set up a tent. You'd be squeezed in on all sides, and the waterline would be packed with so many little kids it would take you forever just to get into the water deep enough to feel the waves against your legs.

Her father had studied the videos taken about Son Doong, either from the official website or YouTube videos from former tourists.

"There, Sally, that's where you and I will swim," he'd said one night, smiling bigger than Sally had ever seen her father smile. He was tapping his tablet. "I think I know how to get there, too. I will study it. We'll go in with a tour and then sneak away and enjoy a few hours. Make sure you pack your bathing suit."

Sally had packed the one-piece she hated, not the new two-piece that showed off her new curves. She was a late bloomer but now she had some of the boys looking her way when they thought she wasn't noticing.

I'm a woman, Sally thought as she swam.

Her father had initially joined her in the water, laughing and splashing like a child. He raced her back and forth until he was exhausted, finally climbing out of the water and telling Sally she had a few more minutes until they needed to dry off and get dressed. They'd worn their swimsuits under their normal clothing.

Her mother hated swimming. Sally couldn't remember her ever getting into a pool, preferring to sit nearby and relax. Watch Sally as she swam.

"Don't go too far," her mother said again, louder.

Sally's father shooshed his wife. He was in fear they'd be caught and either thrown out and banned from Son Doong, or arrested.

"You don't want to go to prison in a foreign country," Sally's father would say.

Her mother had chuckled. "Or in a New York prison, either."

Sally swam and swam, loving the cool water. It was hot and humid in Vietnam, like an awful summer day in Brooklyn. She was going to stay in the water as long as she could.

Until I want to get out, Sally thought. *I'm an adult and I make my own decisions*.

Like when she went back to Brooklyn, she was going to go right up to Miguel before the first period and kiss him. That was it. She knew he liked her, and she liked him. Why was she so scared to talk to him about it, or to make the first move? All of her friends had said she was chicken. They'd dared her to do it before she left for vacation, but Sally hadn't had the right moment. Miguel was always around his boys, talking about sports and laughing.

Monday morning she was going to do it. No words needed to be spoken, just a quick kiss on his lips. Sally had never kissed a boy before.

No, Miguel is a man and I am a woman, she thought, smiling.

Her mother was yelling something, but the words were muffled.

Sally turned to see she was very far away now, lost in her thoughts and swimming.

How far have I gone? Too far, Sally thought. She glanced back the way she was going to see if she could find the other side. Maybe she was closer to shore on this side and could walk back to her parents, although she preferred swimming it.

Her arms were getting tired, though.

Sally thought she saw a light ahead, not too far.

She swam toward it, ignoring her mother for the moment. As she swam closer, she saw it was a natural light, like glowing lichens. Covering only a small part of the wall just above the surface of the pool on the ceiling, which had begun to lower now that she moved closer.

The glow was bright enough she could see strange markings on the ceiling, inches above her head. Sally wasn't claustrophobic but all of that earth above her head gave her pause.

She could hear her mother shouting again, the words echoing off of all the rock.

There was a ledge near the glowing lichen, and Sally pulled herself up onto it, resting her arms. She felt like she was playing Minecraft, finding a hidden world below the surface.

Sally couldn't see her parents from where she was sitting, but she didn't really care. This was some nice alone time. The hotel they were staying in was one room, so she was constantly bumping into either parent, and there was no privacy except if she went into the bathroom.

Exploring the small area a bit, Sally was surprised to see more light a few feet away, which she hadn't seen from her angle in the water. She scooted over, the rocks wet and cold, until she was next to the source of the light, which was what looked like a cave entrance.

Sally smiled. She would see what was inside and have a great story for her parents. For Miguel next week when she was back in school, too. Her future boyfriend would love this story, Sally was sure of it.

There were strange carvings on the walls, all around the small opening. With the glow of the lichens they seemed odd but not scary. Sally wished she had her phone with her so she could take pictures.

Sally was disappointed to see there was a large group of rocks blocking the entrance within a few feet.

I can turn back and tell my parents what I saw, which wasn't much, or I can see if I can yank some rocks away and go deeper, Sally thought.

Right now there wasn't much of a story. She'd say she found a blocked tunnel and… that was it. Not much to tell, and not enough to impress her new boyfriend, Miguel.

Sally started to pry the stones away, one at a time. They were wedged in but it was like a puzzle, and as she found the next looser one, the others shifted slightly and she was able to get fingers into the cracks and pull the rock free.

There was another noise, maybe her mother calling again, but with the echo in the small space it sounded like it had come from inside the tunnel.

Sally stopped. What if there was a wild animal inside? Maybe she was disturbing the den of a bear? She didn't even know if there were bears in Vietnam.

Now she wished she'd listened to her father's many talks about Vietnam, the culture and the fauna and the wildlife. The customs she needed to make sure she was on the right side of, and what food she should and shouldn't eat.

It was easier for Sally to do things in front of her parents and let them tell her if she was doing it wrong or was about to do something harmful. Not that everything was so different in Vietnam and Brooklyn was the opposite.

Sally enjoyed Vietnamese food, having gone after school with friends a few times. There was a very delicious dish she usually ordered, but now she couldn't remember the name of it.

Since nothing had attacked her, Sally crouched down and moved into the cave mouth. There were no more lichens inside so it was pitch black.

I should go back and tell my parents, Sally thought.

That was one of her last thoughts, as the darkness in front of her seemed to shift and move.

It turned into a set of small black hairy hands with tremendous strength, yanking Sally into the hole with such force she was slammed against the side and lost consciousness.

CHAPTER TWO

Vinh Luong frowned and shook his head. This was worse than he'd initially thought. No one had told him the missing teenager was an American. It would be bad enough if a local girl had gone into Son Doong and was missing, but this added an extra wrinkle.

This could turn into an international incident, one his country didn't need.

He was a senior officer of the Vietnam People's Public Security and assigned to the case within hours of the girl going missing.

Her parents were off to the side with another officer, and he could see the distress on their faces.

Now Vinh knew why he'd been assigned, too. He'd spent his teen years and most of his twenties in the United States. First, as a student and then in north Florida as a police officer with JSO, Jacksonville Sheriff's Office. After an incident he'd retired and moved back to Vietnam to be with his family, wanting nothing more to do with the politics behind the police force.

He'd been with the Vietnam People's Police for nearly ten years, after wasting a lot of months trying other jobs that didn't fit his particular skill set.

"Do you speak English?"

Vinh turned to see what was likely the father of the missing girl. He looked upset, which was fitting, since his daughter was gone.

I speak better English than you do, fool, Vinh thought. He forced a quick smile to his face and nodded. "Indeed I do, Mister Rodriquez. You'll find most of us speak it quite well."

The man looked relieved. "My daughter is missing."

"Which is why I'm here… to help you locate her safe and sound." Vinh motioned for the man to walk with him, so they could talk without too many ears. He was sure, even though he was heading this investigation, there would be those more loyal to the bosses than to justice trying to gather as much information as possible.

Vinh knew everyone above his pay grade had their own agenda, and he wasn't included in any of it unless it benefited them.

"Where and when did you last see her?" Vinh asked, trying to seem calm but authoritative. The last thing he needed was some snooty American to either tell him how to do his job or to think he wasn't competent enough to do it.

Mister Rodriquez frowned but turned and pointed. "In the water."

"Why was she in the water?" Vinh tried not to look annoyed, but he already knew this was going to be worse than he'd thought.

Maybe they've given me this mess because they're trying to hang me out to dry, he thought. Vinh knew more than half of his superiors didn't trust him, especially after the investigation a few months ago. The whispers of him being a spy for the Chinese had finally stopped, or had been so low lately he didn't hear them. Regardless, he just wanted to do his job, get paid and try to enjoy his free time.

"Okay, okay… we went for a swim," the man said.

"Why? There are plenty of signs about it being illegal to swim down here. They're even in English, so there's no excuse," Vinh said.

"Look… Sally is missing. We need to find her."

Vinh nodded. "It would help if you showed me exactly where she was when you last saw her, a general idea how far out before she went under."

The man shook his head. "No. She swam out and I lost sight of her. It's really dark after a bit, you know?"

"Maybe she's on the other side or found another tunnel and is in another cavern," Vinh said. He was losing patience. This man's daughter was wandering Son Doong while he was wasting his time asking questions. “I’m sure she’ll show up soon.”

The man looked annoyed. “That’s it? You’re not going to look for her?”

Vinh sighed. Americans were always so pushy, even though he’d lived in their country for so many years. Always getting what they wanted without regard for anyone else. “I didn’t say that, sir. We are going to look for her. Obviously.” He turned and saw Thu Pham, a colleague who’d just arrived at the scene.

Their eyes met and Vinh was happy he didn’t look away first. The two of them had flirted a bit at first, but Thu had cooled off a lot in the last few months, right around the time Vinh was being accused of being a traitor to Vietnam.

Vinh had work to do and waved her over. She walked over and stood stock-still in front of him, making eye contact without blinking. A consummate professional.

“This is Mister Rodriquez. He says his daughter, Sally, swam out and he lost her. We’ll need a boat and a couple of divers. Maybe shut down the caves or at least this area. Got it?”

Thu nodded and turned on her heels, talking on her radio as she moved.

“See? Boats and divers are going to find your daughter, if she’s in the lake.” Vinh didn’t want to mention the idea that she could be dead already, drowned or trapped in a cave without an exit.

You never told people that, especially if they were Americans. They tended to get very emotional, which made Vinh uneasy as well as put too much focus on their pain from everyone. The people who should be trying to find their daughter's body in the underground lake.

Vinh tried to put on a sympathetic face. He could easily arrest the man for going into the water, since there were signs within viewing no matter where you looked. It was because of incidents like this it was illegal to enter the lake.

Instead, he simply walked away and attempted to set up a command center area, telling the officers nearby to keep the crowds back. Make sure the tourists kept following the path and stayed with their guides.

Vinh didn't want anyone around when they pulled the girl's body from the lake, and he knew it was going to happen. She didn't find another exit and wasn't swimming around enjoying herself with all this commotion on the shore.

She was definitely dead.

Vinh hoped the family didn't break down loudly when it happened, when a diver dragged the lifeless corpse from the water.

He knew his thoughts were insensitive, but they were his true feelings. He'd been around a lot of dead bodies in his career. It wasn't fun and it never made you comfortable, but it was part of the job. You either faced it without fear and were practical about it, or you didn't last long in this line of work.

It made sense to keep his feelings to himself, of course. Even when talking to his fellow officers. He didn't exactly trust anyone. He knew they looked at him funny, talked behind his back, because he'd been in the United States. They weren't exactly the enemy, but it was an uneasy alliance.

The Vietnamese people took the U.S. dollars. They smiled and made their money, like most tourist areas learned to do. There was an underlying dislike, though, and Vinh understood it. He was treated differently while working in the U.S. and because of his involvement there, he was treated differently here. In his home country.

He knew he'd never win, so he needed to make the most of it.

Thu came over to Vinh and dropped her voice to a whisper. "What do we really think is going on?"

Vinh tried not to frown but failed. "Not everything is a conspiracy theory. The stupid girl and her stupid father went into the water and she drowned. Case closed. Find the body so we can all be home for dinner."

"Not them," Thu said, glancing at the distraught parents.

"Maybe follow the rules, especially when you're in a foreign country." Vinh caught himself. He didn't need to be so emotional, so cruel, especially in front of Thu. He didn't trust her. She'd been looked over for promotion several times in the past couple of years, even though she was very good at her job.

Vinh had the feeling she resented him coming back home and immediately being her superior, a position she'd been fighting for.

Not that he didn't think he deserved it, mind you. Vinh was very good at what he did, much better than anyone else he worked with.

Thu was good but she'd never be on a level he was, even on his worst day and her best.

Still, he knew he needed to play the game. Move up the ranks and make more and more money and gather whatever else he needed.

"Hopefully the girl is still alive. Passed out on a rock deep into the lake, or she found another tunnel and is lost but alive." Vinh didn't believe any of that nonsense, but he needed to be positive. Not for the family but so Thu would back off and get back to her job.

"We'll see. The divers should be in the water within half an hour," Thu said. She walked away, and Vinh thought she'd looked at him sideways before leaving.

Vinh was getting hungry. He hoped someone had the bright idea to order in some food, but he wasn't going to be that person. It would seem callous coming from him.

As an officer walked past, Vinh stopped him. "See if the father or mother needs something to eat or drink. We should probably have them seated in our command tent so they can feel like they're part of this." Vinh frowned when he saw the officer looking at him strangely. "Part of the process of finding their daughter is what I mean."

"Of course."

Vinh watched as the man walked over and led the couple to the main tent.

His stomach growled. This was going to be a long day and likely night, too.

Unless they found the girl's body quickly and could pack all of this up and go on with their lives.

CHAPTER THREE

Giang came back up and waited for the other divers to surface. They'd hit the bottom of the lake a couple of times already, searching in the many small openings and even found a couple of caves but there was no body inside either of them.

He went down again as soon as two other divers came up, giving them a thumbs up to let them know. The lights on either shoulder offered only a few feet in front of Giang to see.

The sediment had been churned up enough that there was low visibility in places, but Giang could figure out where he'd been in the search.

He started at the nearest wall and moved to his right. They hadn't gone more than halfway across the lake so far and Giang was the lead diver, so he set the pace and the zones.

They'd done this a hundred times in the past ten years, and had a perfect record for finding bodies, weapons tossed in the water or vehicles that had been dumped in a river or lake.

Finding a body was hard and Giang knew, when the girl was found, he'd have nightmares for weeks. He never drank alcohol except a few nights after finding some waterlogged corpse. Then he'd need a couple of days off from work, and he'd close all the blinds and dive into a bottle of whiskey or bourbon.

His wife knew better than to disturb him. Not that he'd get violent or nasty, but he'd further shut down if she tried to talk to him about it.

Giang pushed away his morbid thoughts about finding the girl's corpse. He needed to be more positive. Put it out in the world. That's what he was supposed to do, so the girl would be found alive.

Unharmed.

He followed the natural curve of the lake and kept moving, occasionally seeing a faint glow from a nearby diver using their lights to search.

Giang kept in contact with the team, letting them know where he was and the path he was following so one diver would follow his path, more or less, and make sure he didn't miss a clue, while the rest would do the same doubling up in another lane.

A search this big could take anywhere from six to ten hours, depending on how many caves and hiding places there might be.

Giang knew this was going to push the ten hour limit, because there was so much to explore.

At least there aren't any creatures swimming with us, Giang thought.

He'd been to many countries to help search for people or items, and the worst places were the murky rivers, where you could be attacked by crocodiles, sharks, catfish, eels and a dozen other predators who didn't appreciate you in their territory.

Underground lakes usually had small creatures in it, mostly blind shrimp being the biggest he'd seen. He'd heard of other divers being attacked by bigger sea life, and his wife and Giang had laughed through a movie they'd rented about a giant, blind albino shark living in underwater ruins. It had been mindless fun and nothing more. He'd kept his mouth shut when the divers did things that made no sense, and reality would've been nice for a few scenes.

"I think I have something," a diver said.

"Everyone keep searching and I'll come to you," Giang said. No sense in the team breaking away from where they were and then having to find their spot again. While they used tracking software, it wasn't perfect. It would give you a rough idea of where you'd been but not to the inch, or even sometimes to within five feet. The government would eventually have to update this archaic software, but until then the divers mostly tried their best to do their job.

Giang swam across the lake. He knew if the body had been found they had code words for it. No sense in alerting anyone listening in on their communications before they had time to figure out if they'd found the person and in what condition it was in.

The worst he'd ever found was what ended up being ruled a boating accident. A drunk woman fell off the stern of the boat and was cut to ribbons in the twin motors, shredding her. The blood alerted every shark in the water, and they made a quick meal of most of her body before she was found and pulled out.

There wasn't much left of her to make a true identification. Even her teeth had been eaten by a shark, but she was the only person who'd gone into the water in that area.

Giang had fallen into a whiskey bottle for three days on that one, only surfacing when he was needed with another operation.

Instead of speaking, they liked to also use hand signals when they were underwater. Giang knew the government was listening and recording everything they did, so they could refer to it or likely use it against the dive team if something went wrong. He might be paranoid, but it didn't mean he was wrong.

Not what we're looking for, but interesting, the diver said through hand signals.

It was a broken speargun perched on a rock shelf just below the diver who'd found it.

Not what they were looking for, but interesting enough. Who would be down here using a speargun, when there weren't any creatures big enough to use it on?

Maybe someone was practicing with it, Giang thought. Not that it made any sense. There were a million other places to use it.

Giang motioned for the diver to bag and tag it. They'd hand it over to the authorities and let them worry about it.

He swam back over to the area he'd been searching, popping up out of the water to see how far he'd come and where the shoreline was behind them.

A faint glow on the far wall caught his eye. He swam toward it, even though it wasn't in the lane he'd been following. Giang made a mental note to get back to his area as soon as he figured out who was ahead of him, if it was another diver. By the faint glow of the light, he doubted it was one of his team.

Giang wanted to get some backup, but he wasn't sure why. His gut told him this was going to be something strange, something unexpected, and he might need a second set of eyes on whatever it turned out to be.

Instead, he kept swimming toward the glow.

On the other side there was a natural ledge he was able to stand on and see around a large outcropping of rock. The glow was prominent from this angle, and it looked natural.

A fungus or moss growing on the rocks in places, giving off a faint light.

Giang pulled himself up and saw a path, well-worn and dusty, leading past the glowing moss. Whatever it was.

I should call for backup, Giang thought. He hesitated. Maybe he could find the girl on his own. She'd likely found her way here, guided by the light, and was now wandering through the cave systems.

Giang moved forward and saw what looked like a disturbance. A bunch of small rocks had been moved from what looked like a tunnel.

He looked back in the water, hoping to see one of his crew nearby, but the lake was dark. With such poor visibility, they could be ten feet below the surface and he'd never be able to see them.

Giang groaned. He knew he was supposed to have someone else with him if possible, but it wasn't a written law. It was just what made sense being on these searches.

He glanced at the tunnel again. Took a few steps forward and had a long look as far as his shoulder lights could penetrate the darkness.

There was nothing he could see out of place, although he was sure the ground had been disturbed in a couple of places and he might be seeing footsteps in the dust and dirt.

I need to let the authorities know what I've found, Giang thought. He took another step forward and then stopped.

Giang might contaminate the area in the event the girl was no longer alive. Maybe she found the tunnel and began to walk down it, but fell into a crevasse and died. He doubted she had a flashlight with her, since they'd been swimming.

The glowing stuff on the rocks didn't extend into the cave, so it was a safe bet to Giang that even if the girl had gone this way, she'd be lost within a few feet.

Giang might need to find her quickly. Perhaps she was only a few feet inside the cave, unconscious and still alive. Hurt and needing care.

He stood at the mouth of the tunnel, leaning forward, noting the footprints inside.

It also looked like other prints, smaller, in the immediate area, too. Did this mean there were wild animals down here, too? Giang wasn't too familiar with the history of Son Doong other than what he'd read about online when it had initially been discovered. He didn't remember mention of wild animals being found, either.

He was sure the occasional howling monkey or bat was inside the cave system, and might even remember reading about them at some point.

Giang stared down at the many prints, most of them fairly new.

He heard a splash in the water behind him and hoped it was one of his fellow divers, but when he turned back all he saw was a ripple on the surface. No submerged lights.

Giang took a deep breath and composed himself. He decided the best course would be to summon not only another diver but the Vietnam People's Public Security team, too. Let them handle this. That was their job.

If there wasn't a dead body to be pulled from the lake, then his job was done here.

He'd alert the authorities and then keep moving in the lake until she was either recovered in the caves or in the water.

Giang knew his job was to keep searching in the water.

He radioed it in and waited for someone else to arrive, hoping they'd be quick about it.

This area of the lake was creepy. The outcropping blocked sight of the far shore, where everyone had set up to search.

Giang wondered if he'd buy a bottle of whiskey on his way home tonight.

CHAPTER FOUR

Sally couldn't see her hands in front of her face. It was complete darkness, so black all she saw was flashes of light from her mind or her eyes trying to decipher what was happening.

She'd been snatched by something, or a few somethings. Dragged into the tunnel and banged around until she'd hit her head and passed out.

Not knowing how long she'd been unconscious, all she could do was clear her head and figure out where she was and how to escape.

She felt like a prisoner of whatever had clubbed and dragged her into the tunnel.

Sally was resting against a hard surface, likely a rock wall.

Her hearing adjusted and she could hear scurrying around her, but it was distant. Maybe. It was hard to tell, or figure out how big of a space she was in, without moving.

As soon as she tried to stand she tapped her head on the roof, but not too hard she was knocked out again.

Feeling with her hands, she felt the irregular wall on either side.

The ground was also rocky, with what she figured was sand.

As soon as she started to move the sounds around her stopped.

Sally felt the walls around her and when the ceiling slowly rose she was thankful, finally able to stand on her feet. She tried to reach up but she couldn't feel the ceiling after a few steps, which meant she'd been placed into a niche of the cave.

Pacing it slowly, she felt like she was being watched.

Sally thought she heard scuffling behind her but when she turned suddenly there was no sound. It might be in her head.

She walked the room a couple of times, figuring it might be about twenty feet by twenty feet, roughly circular. She couldn't find a tunnel leading out, though.

How had she gotten into this chamber?

Sally began feeling the walls, reaching as high as she could. There might be a ledge above her, but she could only feel it with the tips of her fingers.

Something moved above, where she was reaching, a scraping noise against the rock.

"Hello? Is there someone there?"

Sally heard an intake of breath and then something running away, no longer trying to be quiet.

"Help me. If anyone can hear me, I'm down here," Sally yelled. Maybe her words might be heard by her father. Surely, if she'd been unconscious for longer than a few minutes, a search party might be forming to find her.

If it was a wild animal that dragged her down the tunnel and deposited her in this cave, maybe Sally scared it away with all of the yelling.

She searched for another exit from the cave but couldn't find another one.

Jumping as high as she could, Sally tried to grab onto the ledge and pull herself up.

At first she didn't make it, falling short. Her arms and fingers hurt but she knew she couldn't give up. Sally managed to leap and get both hands onto some cracked rock, digging her fingers into a small crevasse.

She pulled herself up and managed to swing her legs up and over.

Wearing only a bathing suit, Sally knew she was going to get torn up. Already her hands felt scratched and she knew they'd be bloody soon enough.

Just by the noise she knew this area was smaller than the room she'd come out of, but she had no idea if it was simply a rock ledge or a genuine way out. Sally had tried to find the spot where she thought she heard the animal or person, and felt like she was at the spot.

Sally raised her hand and felt the rocky ceiling above, no more than a couple of feet. She took her time, trying not to panic, feeling around to gauge how big the area was.

There was a slight breeze coming from in front of her, and Sally began shuffling toward it. Her knees and arms were getting scraped up pretty good, but the adrenaline of escaping was keeping her moving. She knew, if she got out of the cave system, she'd sleep for days.

Not if. When, Sally thought, trying to stay positive.

She thought she found an exit and began crawling faster, knowing she needed to slow down but unable to make that common sense move work right now. It was time to get back to her parents, time to feel safe again.

Sally felt solid rock in front of her and knew this was a dead end.

Groaning, she shifted to go back the way she'd come, hoping she'd missed another tunnel back behind her.

Sally stopped when she heard something shuffling behind her, too close for comfort.

"Hello? Is anybody there?"

She counted to ten in her head but there were no other noises.

"Please don't eat me," Sally said and smiled, more as a morbid joke than anything else. She knew her nerves were frazzled.

Sally started to crawl again, careful not to end up back at the room she'd woken up in and fall back into it.

Her hands were feeling the walls on either side and to her right she encountered only air.

Sally slid closer to it and found another tunnel, and it seemed wider. How had she missed it going the other way?

She took a couple of deep breaths. The air was still and stagnant down here, or over here, or where she currently was. She felt like there were miles and miles of rocks above her head, threatening to let gravity push it all down on her head.

There was another slight breeze she felt, and she decided it could be the way out.

Sally tried to remain calm and keep moving slowly and surely, but it was tough to do when freedom could be a few feet away.

Her hands were rough and she might be bleeding, which wasn't good. If there was an animal nearby, stalking her, it might have an easy blood trail to follow.

Sally moved for what felt like half a mile, on her hands and knees, before she felt the space open up. It was more a feeling than actually knowing, until she lifted her hand and couldn't feel the roof of the tunnel anymore.

She stood and listened. There was water dripping ahead of her but it sounded far away and echoed. Sally started to shuffle her feet forward, careful not to trip and fall.

Without light she had no clue how far she walked until her hand hit another solid wall. She'd crossed a large cavern and began to feel to her left, hoping to find another exit to continue her escape.

Escape from what, exactly? She couldn't remember much after finding the tunnel when she'd swam across the lake. Had she banged her head and fallen down a shaft, finally ending up in that room?

Sally wondered if a wild animal or a pack of animals had found her unconscious and dragged her through endless tunnels, depositing her there to eat at a later date.

The idea of being a future meal for an animal capable of eating her wasn't a pleasant thought. She was cold, her bathing suit still wet, and she was barefoot. She knew her feet would be torn up by the time she got back to her family.

A small price to pay for freedom, Sally thought.

She worried her parents were losing their minds not knowing where she was. Surely, her father would swim into the lake and look for her.

No. Maybe they think I drowned, she thought.

It was a sobering thought. Sally knew she was everything to her parents, and at times growing up she wondered if they were still together only because of her. She'd never seen them being affectionate to one another. They never fought, but they never had any real passion, either.

Trips and large gifts were everything to her parents, the showing of material things instead of affection.

Sally was showered by both of them, and she knew at times it was more of a rivalry than pure love. They wanted to know everything she was doing, be a part of her life.

As she got older, Sally knew it was smothering and there'd be a time when she'd have to push back. She didn't bother inviting her friends over for sleepovers, because she knew her parents would end up hanging out watching movies with them or other embarrassing things.

If she were being honest, she had only a few real friends. Only a few acquaintances and she only talked to them at school.

Her parents were too nosy, too in her business.

Sally wondered why she was even thinking about any of this as she tried to find a way forward, a way out of this room.

Her hand hit nothing but air and she got excited, feeling a slight breeze.

Sally slid closer and felt another wall, only inches away. This was not an exit, but a crack in the wall. She groaned and tried to follow it blindly with her hand, hoping it led to a larger exit.

She didn't find an opening big enough for her body, and kept feeling the walls as she moved.

When she finally found an opening, she paused.

Was this the one she'd originally come into from the opposite direction?

Sally wanted to cry.

CHAPTER FIVE

Giang had called for backup ten minutes ago. He'd been treading water, waiting for someone else to arrive.

"Have you found anything?" Giang asked over his radio, but all he received back was static. Maybe no one had even heard his call for more help.

Groaning, he moved in a wide circle on the surface, hoping to either see other divers below or eventually find a spot to rest or have gone back to the beginning, when he'd step out of the lake and ask for some help.

He ended up back at the shelf he'd spotted and decided to hop up out of the water and rest. His arms and legs were getting heavy from all of the swimming.

Giang could get a better look at the tunnel he'd seen, too, and the glowing lichen.

He tried the radio again but only got more static.

The smart move is for me to swim back to shore and get help, Giang thought.

He decided to explore a bit before he dove back into the water.

Giang took off his excess equipment and laid it out on the ridge, away from the water. Not that he thought it would accidentally fall in or get stolen, but better safe than sorry.

It was still within sight, so if anyone came upon it, the equipment wouldn't be hidden. He had his name on most of the pieces since they were owned by him.

He walked the shelf, bending down a few times to see if he could detect footprints or anything exciting.

Except for some rocks, there was nothing of interest.

Giang walked the ledge to the end before turning back and going the opposite way.

The glow of lichen gave him more than enough light, even though he had his waterproof torch.

"What? Huh," Giang said when he noticed the fingerprints in the lichen, scraped against the wall. It had been disturbed and nearly destroyed, but some small amount remained of the glowing fungi.

Is it a fungus? I need to look that up when I get home, Giang thought.

There was a tunnel and he stooped down and saw footprints in the dirt, as well as scratches on the lower portion of the walls on either side. Maybe an animal was inside, like a den.

Now is the time to get back in the water and get some help, Giang thought.

He hesitated. What if the missing girl was only a few feet away, unconscious? Maybe an animal had dragged her inside after she bumped her head or nearly drowned. She could be in need right now, not an hour from now.

"Hello? Sally? Can you hear me?" Giang said loudly, hoping the girl would hear him. If nothing else, any animals might flee. He'd hate to be attacked down here. Who knew what creatures made their home in these tunnels.

Giang took three steps inside and paused, listening for a response from Sally or animals fleeing.

He heard nothing, but the sound of the water lapping onto the ledge behind him made it difficult to hear any small noise.

Using his torch, he tried to see as far down the tunnel as he could, but it sloped downward after only a few feet. Could the girl have entered in the darkness and slipped down the tunnel and just out of sight?

Giang rubbed at the remaining lichen on the wall until it was nearly gone, smudges left. There were tracks in the dust and dirt leading into the tunnel as far as he could see, and he knew time was of the essence.

Any lost minute and Sally could be dead or dying, and he might be only a few feet away from her.

Giang called out to her again but didn't hear a response. Maybe she was too far inside the cave system to hear or she was unconscious.

He took a few steps inside the tunnel, sweeping his light back and forth so he didn't miss any clues as to her whereabouts.

Except for many footprints of various animals, Giang couldn't see much else. If Sally had come this way, which was likely, she hadn't dropped anything. Not that he supposed she was carrying much, since she should be in her bathing suit and she was swimming in the underground lake.

Giang was maybe thirty feet into the tunnel. It had sloped down but it wasn't a steep drop-off, which was good. Just enough to let you know it curved down. Easy enough to navigate.

Again, he hesitated. He should wait for backup or swim back across the lake and wave to the other searchers so they could help him.

Time might be running out for poor Sally, Giang thought.

He kept moving forward, trying to be quiet so he could hear if Sally was nearby and hurt. He hoped she was not, only frightened and curled up against a wall somewhere not too farther away.

"Sally? Can you hear me?" Giang called out after a few more steps. The ground underfoot was no longer marked with dirt or dust. Not that it was necessarily clean, but it wasn't covered enough to show any marks or footprints.

A hundred feet down the tunnel Giang could see it split to the left and to the right.

He'd need to make a decision, either to follow one of the paths or turn back and get help.

His mind was screaming to get help but he knew he'd need to be the hero and find Sally. It was part of his charm, and the curse of being him. He always needed to succeed, especially when no one had faith he could do it.

Giang decided to go left for about a hundred feet and then turn back and go the other way. Do some searching. If he didn't find anything he swore he'd go back and get more help. These tunnels could run for miles and miles. He was sure no one had properly explored them, and most of Son Doong was still unmapped.

At about a hundred feet Giang stopped. This path continued but he'd called out to Sally again and heard nothing back.

Giang turned around and went back to the crossroads, heading in the other direction. He was hoping someone else might've found the opening by now or at least seen his gear on the ledge outside.

He began walking in the other direction, light moving back and forth as he went.

Giang stopped. Was that a noise he'd heard, briefly, somewhere in the distance?

"Sally? Can you hear me?"

After at least three minutes, when the sound didn't return, Giang began walking again. The problem was the echoes inside the tunnels were very confusing. A drip of water miles away might be coming back, sounding like it was around the next turn. He couldn't trust his ears.

All he could do was keep moving and looking for signs the girl had come this way.

Giang had a sudden worry he'd get lost. He decided it was better to go back and try the radio again.

He called out another couple of times but got no response.

When he turned to go back he thought he saw movement just beyond the light.

"Sally? Hello? Can you hear me? I've come to rescue you," Giang said, stepping forward.

There was no one there and he didn't know if he was starting to see things. While the tunnels were high enough for him to stand in, the walls seemed to be closing in on both sides. There were gaps he had to crouch down or move sideways to pass, and he wasn't a fan of that.

Giang had the unsettling fear he needed to leave but it might be too late.

He turned and started heading back the way he'd originally come into the cave system, moving as fast as he could.

Not thinking he'd made another turn, Giang quickly found himself in a wrong tunnel, one he'd never visited in this brief trip. The floors were dusty and he added the only prints to it.

"I'm lost," Giang mumbled, turning back the way he'd come.

He saw definite movement up ahead, a dark shape just out of reach of his light.

"Hello? Sally? Is that you?" Giang rushed forward, knowing he was close to panicking. Likely, the shadows were playing tricks on him and there was nothing else in these tunnels but him and his imagination.

At another fork in the tunnel, Giang decided to go left. Neither way looked like he'd been down it before, even though he'd seen no other passages and knew he'd had to have come down one of them. He was turned around and confused now, and he felt like he was seconds from screaming for help and collapsing.

Giang shone the light behind him and screamed when a small dark figure appeared as if by magic.

He dropped the torch and it rolled against the wall, shining the light on nothing.

Giang dove to the ground to grab the torch, hoping it wouldn't go out.

Hoping what he'd seen was his imagination, too, because the figure he'd glimpsed wasn't Sally and wasn't anything human.

Giang felt like he was surrounded now. He stumbled to pick up his light source, inadvertently turning it off as he lifted it from the ground.

He groaned and didn't think he'd ever been this scared in his life.

Pressing his back against a wall and glad he'd still had the image in his head of the dimensions of the tunnel, his fingers were twitching and he couldn't get a good grip on the torch to turn it back on.

If he was lucky, whatever he'd seen was either not real or had run off, scared from the light going out. Hopefully even more scared than Giang felt right now.

He flicked the switch and shined the light back and forth.

Instead of an empty tunnel and the knowledge he'd been wrong and he was alone, Giang cried out when the nearest creature, and there were at least a dozen of them, sunk its over-large fangs into his thigh, ripping through his wetsuit with ease.

Giang screamed for the next minute or two, before the dark creatures methodically devoured every last inch of him, down to cracking his bones to dust and licking it up.

CHAPTER SIX

Vinh was worried his main diver, Giang, hadn't checked in in over an hour, but he was never going to panic or let anyone around him know his worries.

"I need a diver who can hear me to also be searching for Giang. I need to talk with him and he seems to be out of range," Vinh said as calmly as he could.

Giang was always a wealth of information during these rescues, and Vinh tried to lean on him as much as possible.

It's not like I'm putting on a wetsuit and going into this icy water, Vinh thought.

The men weren't friends. They'd never go out for a drink after working together. Never be invited to parties or family events. They saw one another only in times like these, times of crisis.

Vinh watched as Thu talked to the parents of the missing girl. She'd do all of the legwork there, getting a second and third interview. Already, there were signs the family had done the unimaginable: they'd purposely put their daughter in danger by ignoring all of the warning posts.

By ignoring common sense, Vinh thought.

He'd wait to bring up criminal charges. Not until they either rescued the daughter or retrieved her body. He would also push for the company responsible for the Son Doong cave systems to file charges as well, because they'd be losing at least a day or two of revenue while the tourist attraction was closed.

Vinh didn't care if the girl was alive or dead, if he were being honest. It would be about the same paperwork. It would also hopefully be a good lesson for future tourists. Maybe they'd obey the warnings, which were posted everywhere. Especially at the initial box office to enter the cave system. Plenty of warnings to read. The booklet they handed you with your ticket also had two full pages of those same warnings on them.

Not that it mattered. Vinh was surprised this was the first time trying to find someone lost in these caves, which ran for miles. Even though they had only recently been discovered and new areas were found all the time, he worried more and more incidents would happen.

Then the Vietnam People's Public Security would create another division, one to only worry about stupid tourists wandering the caves.

Vinh knew he'd be the person tasked with running it, too, because he was here right now. At the beginning of this endless loop of tourists getting lost.

He tried the radio again but it was no use. There were only a few spots he could stand at to get a good enough signal, and it usually came in broken, anyway.

Thu walked over to him with a smile. "He knows he screwed up. They'd planned this trip and the swim for a long time, but he had no idea she could get lost."

"In dark underground water? Really? He had no idea there was such a risk?" Vinh shook his head. "He'd better hope we find his daughter."

"Obviously." Thu frowned. "What do you need from me now?"

"I need a diver to find Giang. I'll need an update from the man," Vinh said. "Can you do that?"

He knew he was on the edge of being quite rude to Thu, but he couldn't help it. He wasn't a fan of the woman or his waste of talent today.

"I'll handle it, sir," Thu said with a frown and quickly turned away.

Vinh knew she was likely rolling her eyes as she strode away, but he didn't care. Her opinion didn't matter to him. No one currently surrounding him was important enough to worry about.

He paced the small beach area, not making eye contact with anyone, as if he was deep in thought about this ongoing case.

In actuality, Vinh was thinking about what he'd have for dinner tonight. He wanted to try out a couple of different places that were new in the tourist district. A Mongolian barbeque looked interesting as well as a Taco Bell. He'd never had fast food Mexican and wanted to at least try it once and see what all the hype was about.

Vinh might also check in with a couple of the working girls if he wasn't too tired. It depended on when he got out of these awful caves and what he'd decided on for dinner.

Two divers were coming out of the water and Vinh waved them over.

"Well? Anything?" Vinh asked.

Both men shook their heads. "No sign of the girl. The lake is deep and we found at least two underwater tunnels that might lead to other parts of the system. Heck, they might go all the way to the ocean."

Vinh didn't want to hear that. If they didn't find the girl's body soon, he might be here for the next couple of days. No break, no Taco Bell, no women of the night.

"Did you get in touch with Giang?" Vinh asked.

Both men shook their heads.

"Then get back in the water and find him. Now." Vinh had nearly screamed it and knew all eyes were now on him.

"Uh, yes, sir… we just need new air tanks."

"Hurry up. I need Giang to report to me and the girl found." Vinh almost said he wanted the girl's body found, but knew everyone was listening to him. He turned and addressed the many people standing around. "Do you have a specific job to do, or are you just going to gawk? If you're not helping with the rescue then you need to leave the scene. Immediately."

A few people turned away, as if they were invisible.

Vinh waved for a couple of men he knew were loyal to him. "I want every person in this cave checked and vetted. Got it? If they have no legitimate reason to be here then escort them out. There are too many onlookers and not enough action."

Thu approached. "We have two rescue boats and crews arriving shortly."

"They should've been here initially. Why the delay?" Vinh asked.

Thu looked away. "The divers were called first. I wasn't sure a boat team would be needed, and they were across the city. As soon as I realized-"

"As soon as you realized a girl's life was at stake you decided to do the proper thing, is that it?" Vinh groaned. "Her life isn't important to you. Why? Because she's a foreigner, a tourist? Is this personal, Thu?"

Vinh knew he was grasping at straws but he couldn't help it. She'd cornered herself with this thinking, even if he would've likely done the same thing. Why not think the divers would quickly find her, right? But this would make it easier to go higher up the chain of command and make Thu look incompetent and foolish. With any luck, she'd be knocked down a rung or two on the ladder and not be breathing down his neck in the future.

"No, not personal. I just… I thought that's what you wanted, based on working with you in the past," Thu said. "My mistake."

"Huge mistake. In fact, it could be a fatal one," Vinh said and turned his back to her, letting the woman know he was disappointed and she was in trouble. "Find the girl, Thu."

Vinh heard Thu running away from him and it made him smile.

He hoped the new team would get here soon and rescue this girl or at least find her waterlogged body. He had more important things to do.

A diver came out of the water shaking his head.

"Here," Vinh yelled and waved the man over, before anyone else could talk to him. "Did you find her? Where is Giang?"

Vinh already knew by the look on the man's face he had no answers, but he wanted to be the first to hear the disappointing news.

“No, sir. Nothing on either.”

Vinh was gritting his teeth now. “Then why are you out of the water? Shouldn’t you be doing your job and finding this poor, lost little girl, and finding out why Giang went radio silent, too? He could be trapped in a cavern and running out of air.”

The diver held up his air tank. “I’m out, too. I need to change to a full one. Only be a minute.”

“Then get back in the water,” Vinh said. He saw Thu talking to a couple of other officers and waved her over. He wasn’t going to go to her, let her do the walking so he could show her he was in charge.

She nearly jogged to him, which made Vinh happy. “Yes, sir?”

“I want every diver in the water. Now. Find more divers from neighboring police stations if possible. You dropped the ball by not bringing in the boat crew, and we’re wasting time. This underground lake is too big for a couple of divers to search. I also want someone to find Giang.”

Vinh didn’t know why Giang not being in contact was bothering him so much. Maybe because if the lead diver was running the show in the lake it would free Vinh to act like he was doing some actual work and not have to do actual work. Coordinating all of these moving parts was starting to get on his last nerve.

Thu ran off to hopefully find more divers and Vinh watched as the diver out of the water changed tanks and dove back into the lake.

He wasn't even sure how many divers were currently in the water. He assumed they'd be coming out one at a time to change their air tanks but he was going to make sure they went back into the water as soon as possible.

Vinh wanted this to end.

He stomped back to the command center that had been set up so he could find a chair and sit down, but he stopped halfway across the rocky terrain.

Three men in suits walked down the path, flashing their badges.

Vinh groaned. The Americans had arrived and they'd threaten to take over his crime scene.

Even though he wanted nothing to do with any of this, the thought of these United States government goons blocking him out made him sick to his stomach. He was going to fight them on this, just because he was looking for a fight and a distraction.

Hurry up and pull the girl's lifeless body from the lake, Vinh thought.

CHAPTER SEVEN

Sally felt the slice on her hand a second before she tried to muffle her scream. The pain was excruciating, and when she felt it with her other hand it felt like at least five inches of her thumb down to her wrist had been cut.

Even in the absolute darkness, she knew she was bleeding a lot.

Sally wiped her hand on her bathing suit and tried to press the wound to her thigh so that maybe it would stop bleeding. She wondered how long she could go before she lost too much blood.

With nothing else to do, she kept moving. Trying to feel her way with her good hand and hoping she saw light or the exit to the caves.

There was a shuffling noise behind her, very loud, and she turned. All she saw was a wall of black.

Something is approaching and it doesn't sound like a person, Sally thought.

"Hello? Who's there?" Sally shouted out the words, hoping to scare off a wild animal if that was what was approaching her. She put her back against a wall.

There was something definitely nearby, and she caught a whiff of an animal smell, like a wet dog that hadn't been washed in years.

"Leave me alone," Sally shouted. She knew she needed to keep moving and find her way out but her legs weren't obeying the command from her brain.

Sally raised her bleeding hand over her head, remembering something from school about keeping the cut above her heart. She wasn't sure if that was a real thing or not, but it was worth a shot.

She kept moving, using her good hand to keep from stumbling blindly into a wall and knocking herself out. So far the ground was relatively even, with only some slight dips.

The worry was a huge drop just ahead in the darkness and she'd plunge a hundred feet to her death.

Maybe I deserve to die at this point, Sally thought.

She tried to shake off her thoughts but it was no use. She'd never see her parents again or any of her friends. Never going to graduate high school and college, never land a good job or get married and have kids. Never, ever.

Sally had stopped walking and was leaning against the cold, damp wall of the tunnel and crying now.

The scraping noises were echoing all around her, as if she was surrounded.

"Leave me alone," Sally yelled, lashing out with her good arm.

She hit something short and furry.

Sally screamed and began to run. There was a creature in the tunnel with her, only inches away.

How long she ran she didn't know, but eventually she found herself in a small chamber with no way out but the way she'd come.

If the creature is following me, they have me trapped, Sally thought.

She wished she had a flashlight with her. Even though she'd been down here for so long, her eyes had still not adjusted all too well.

The blackness was impenetrable.

As she found the exit again, Sally knew something was nearby. So close she thought she heard it breathing only a few feet away.

"Hello? What do you want? Can you understand me?" Sally was trying not to shout, talking in measured tones and trying to sound polite. Animals could sense fear. She hoped it was not sensing it from her or seeing her as weak.

Sally shuffled forward. Her hand was still bleeding and she raised it again, putting it on top of her head. She felt the blood trickling into her hair. She wanted to vomit and wondered how long it had been since she'd eaten.

Moving forward again, she wondered if she was simply moving in the same tunnels over and over. In her blind panic she'd likely run down the same path over and over, until she came to this dead end.

Sally decided to take her time now, keeping to the right side of the tunnel. If she could find another opening, maybe she'd be able to find the way out.

How deep and long was this system? Sally felt like she'd walked miles in her bare feet. She didn't want to think about how bad her feet were right now, torn up and missing layers of skin.

The ground was relatively smooth in most places, though. Very rarely had she stepped on a pebble or anything blocking the way.

Did the creature or creatures down here clean up after themselves?

Sally tried to think of little things like that so she could keep moving. Keep processing each minute detail and not the overall thought of her never finding her way out and eventually being eaten by whatever was stalking her.

She had no idea how long she walked but eventually she found another opening to the right and took it, feeling the ground slowly slanting upwards. A good sign.

As she moved she knew she was being followed. Maybe the creature was simply curious.

How long had it been since she'd accidentally touched it? Had to be an hour or two. Time had no meaning down here, though. Sally might be lost for fifteen minutes or fifteen days at this point.

"I'm not going to hurt you," Sally said as nicely as she could.

As if I'm the threat, she thought.

"Maybe we could be friends. Maybe you could lead the way so I can get out of here." Sally knew she was going to lose her mind if she kept thinking this creature, whatever it was, could understand and help her.

Sally walked further along the tunnel, feeling with her good hand for another opening.

As she moved she felt something bump her leg but she didn't scream, instead moving against the wall and standing still.

She heard scuffling but now it was ahead of her.

Had the creature understood what she was saying? Had it moved ahead of her, to lead her to safety? Sally knew that was nothing more than wishful thinking, but she might as well follow along and see what happened.

If she was going to die there was nothing she could do about it. She had no control of this situation.

The creature was tapping on the wall ahead, moving further away.

Sally started to move again, quickening her pace to keep up. Maybe she was being helped.

Maybe there would be a light at the end of the tunnel.

Sally kept moving, her good arm sometimes feeling other tunnels branching off but stopping long enough to hear where the creature was tapping up ahead.

Leading her to safety or her doom.

She was definitely rising, too, each few steps slanting upward. Sally didn't remember how far underground she'd been at the lake, but she guessed they weren't heading back in that direction.

At this point she felt like she had no choice but to follow, stopping every now and then to make sure she hadn't gone the wrong way.

The scraping noises were ahead of her but not too far she couldn't hear them.

Sally was lightheaded and knew she'd lost a lot of blood. She kept forgetting to raise her arm over her head, even though it was starting to hurt her shoulder and her bloody hand on the top of her head felt like it was a hundred pounds pressing down on her skull.

She stumbled over something on the ground and fell, landing on her hands.

Her injured hand felt like it was now on fire, and she screamed in agony. The pain shot up her arm and shook her body. It was so powerful.

Sally fought not to puke. She was dizzy and closed her eyes, trying to let the nausea pass.

When she tried to push up with her good hand she felt something weird on the ground in front of her.

The smell hit her a second later: blood.

By the stench it was a lot of blood, too. Sally pulled her hand away, knowing it was covered in it now.

Sally turned her head and puked, letting it all out. Her body was shaking when she finally stopped. Her ribs hurt. As she stood she kicked something on the ground and reluctantly got down on her knees to figure out what it was in the dark.

It felt like a person. Even though she couldn't see, she just knew.

A dead person who'd been ripped apart and had his or her blood spilled on the ground.

Sally felt like she was going to vomit again, but only bile came back up.

She heard the clicking of the nails in the distance and knew she was being summoned to follow.

Whoever was dead on the ground hadn't been dead for too long. She decided to feel around and see if there was a weapon or anything she could use, but in the dark everything felt strange. He was wearing a wetsuit. That's what it felt like to Sally.

The scraping against the wall sounded again and Sally thought it was closer. Impatient.

"I'm coming. Hold on," Sally said.

She wiped the spittle from her lips and chin. Her hand was throbbing in pain but she didn't know what to do. If she'd had a light source maybe she could find a strip of the wetsuit to use as a tourniquet.

Instead, she followed the sound of nails against the rock, hoping she wasn't stupidly being led to her death.

CHAPTER EIGHT

Hai found Giang's gear on the shelf and sighed. If the man had discarded his gear, it meant he was now searching on land or his gear had stopped working.

Maybe he'd run out of air and got confused as to which way was back to the shore and the command center.

Hai tried to use his radio but he got nothing but static.

Sitting on the shelf with his flippers still in the water, Hai took off his own gear and took in a breath of the stale cavern air. With the lake it made everything wet and slimy, which was not fun.

He needed to get his bearings and figure out exactly where he was. No use in walking around blindly on the shelf, looking for Giang.

"Hello? Giang? Sally? Can anyone hear me? I'm Hai. A diver. I'm here to help," he shouted. The words echoed off of the walls and the low ceiling but he waited and didn't get a response back.

Giang's gear was neatly piled, so Hai knew it hadn't been done under duress or stress. He'd found this shelf and went to explore it.

Hai tried his radio again, asking for help. He figured out the coordinates as best he could on his equipment and marked it so that anyone getting the signal would be able to follow.

While he waited to get into contact with any other diver or Giang, he slowly stripped off his gear. He made sure they were piled neatly next to Giang's items.

He stood and stretched, hands touching the ceiling inches from his head. The ground was wet and looked slippery, but he knew he could manage without falling. Hopefully.

Hai had his torch lit and was shining it in all directions. He also made sure his large knife was at his side, since you never knew what you'd encounter in such a remote area, only recently discovered.

The ledge wasn't as slippery as he thought it would be, but he used his free hand to lean against the wall whenever possible.

Hai only got a few feet before he saw the opening to what was obviously a tunnel. Perhaps even a system of tunnels and caverns. He wished he'd had more time to research Son Doong to see what they'd managed to map and what was still a mystery.

Peering into the tunnel, he thought he saw a disturbance in the dirt on the ground. Maybe footprints. Could it be Giang? Maybe even Sally.

Giang might've followed the initial prints into the cave.

On both walls was a faintly glowing lichen. Hai didn't want to touch it but he got close to it and felt dizzy. It gave off a faint… pulse? It was odd.

He decided to not enter the cave. Not yet. Better to be cautious and have some backup.

"Is there anybody listening?" Hai asked into his radio.

Nothing. No response.

Hai trudged back to his equipment. He thought it best to get his gear back on and swim directly toward the main shore, radioing as he moved for help.

As he got his tank on and was pulling his mask back down, he heard a disturbance in the water nearby.

Bubbles were rising to the surface and Hai watched them with his torch.

A diver popped his head up, looking around.

"Hey," Hai said.

The diver swam over and got up on the ledge with Hai.

"I couldn't get a signal in this part of the lake," the diver said. He extended a hand. "I'm Colin."

Hai smiled and shook the man's hand. "You're not Vietnamese. British?"

Colin nodded. "I'm with the collective Coast Guard. They sent me in because I was actually in the area. I said I'd be happy to help."

"Well, you can help me to check out this opening over here. I feel better with some backup," Hai said. "I don't suppose you were able to radio in and let them know your position?"

Colin shook his head.

"The signal is bouncing all over the place or being blocked with all of this rock. I'm not sure how to proceed," Hai said.

Colin was looking at the water. "If one of us goes back it might take half an hour or more. I'm not even sure where we are right now."

Hai agreed. He knew they were far away from their starting point. "Maybe we'll find other divers and can round them up. I don't know what to do."

"There are two of us now. Maybe we leave our gear with this other gear and do some quick exploring. See where that tunnel leads and if we keep an eye on the entrance we can't go wrong. How does that sound?" Colin was already stripping off his gear.

Hai had to agree because the longer they waited and talked about it the longer the girl that was lost remained lost.

Once Colin was ready, both men had their lights shining on the entrance and their knives at the ready.

"There will likely be an animal somewhere. I've run into a few in my work," Hai said.

Colin nodded, giving Hai the lead as the senior diver.

Hai appreciated the man recognizing Hai, but wished the Brit would take the lead just the same.

"Time to save her life," Hai said with a smile. He moved into the cave mouth and mentally noted how smooth it was only a couple of feet inside, as if it had been worn down over countless centuries. He figured the lake level had been much higher in the past, carving out these caverns.

He worried something big and fierce was living here now, and the creature or creatures had gotten the teenager they were looking for.

And where was Giang? Hai knew him as a veteran diver. It seemed odd he would go off on his own, although with the time seeming to expire on Sally, maybe he felt he had no choice.

Or he'd been face to face with the creature or creatures.

Stop getting ahead of yourself and slow down with the imaginary monsters, Hai thought.

The pair moved deeper into the tunnel until it turned slightly and they could no longer see the entrance.

Both of the men frowned.

"We can keep going or we can turn back and get help," Colin said.

"We go another few meters and reevaluate." Hai thought it was a solid plan. He didn't know what they'd do after walking a bit more, though. Keep stopping, talking and wasting time?

Another few feet inside but there was no change. The floor was barren of dirt or dust so there were no footprints.

Their lights shone down pretty far but there was nothing of importance to see. No markings, no scraps of cloth, no bloodstains.

Another few meters and Hai was about to pull up and ask Colin again what he thought when he saw there was a tunnel branching to the right as well.

Colin sighed. "Two choices is not optimal. We might need some help."

Hai had to agree. He put up a hand to listen but there was nothing he could hear, not even water dripping in the distance.

It was quiet. Too quiet.

"Hello? Giang? Sally? Is anyone there that can hear us?" Hai yelled, listening as his words echoed deeper down the line.

Hai turned back to Colin, ready to usher the man back out to the lake so they could get some help.

He stopped when he heard a very low hum that turned into a keening whine, for only a couple of seconds, before it went silent again.

Colin had heard it because his eyes got big and he pointed down the side tunnel.

That was the direction Hai had also heard it.

Colin moved ahead of Hai and into the tunnel, Hai struggling to keep up.

“Wait, wait. I’m trying to catch up,” Hai said.

Colin was still in sight but he was hard to see since his light was shining ahead of him and his body blocking the tunnel, which had shrunk as they moved.

Hai watched as the light turned to the left and rose slightly before only a quick flash or two was seen.

He came around the turn and stopped short.

On the ground of the tunnel was the flashlight, cracked and off.

Hai hadn’t heard anything abnormal, but he’d been running and panting as he moved.

“Colin? Where are you?” Hai took another step, intending to bend down and pick up the flashlight.

Just beyond his own light’s beam reach he saw something move, but when he raised the light it was gone.

Had he imagined something? Where had Colin gone?

Another few steps forward, broken light forgotten underfoot, and Hai had to stop again.

He’d found Colin.

Dead. Body lying on his side, throat slashed open and blood pooling around his head.

Hai saw the look of horror on Colin's eyes.

"No. This can't be happening," Hai said, fighting the bile down his throat and turning to escape. There was danger here and it was going to get him next.

Something fell from the ceiling, smashing into his arm and knocking the flashlight to the ground, where it spun in a lazy circle, casting shadows and surreal images.

Images that couldn't be real to Hai.

Teeth and fangs. Dark matted hair and a smell of rotting flesh.

Hai felt something dig into his back but when he turned he realized it was hanging onto him.

There was a flash of a razor or maybe a claw near his face.

Hai felt his hot blood pouring from his throat but when he reached up to try to stop the bleeding it was too late.

He died before he hit the ground.

CHAPTER NINE

Vinh shrugged his shoulders. He hadn't actually said a word to the three agents, who'd flashed their department of Homeland Security badges at anyone within ten feet of them.

"We need an update on what has transpired so far," DHS Agent Johnson said, obviously the leader of the trio. He was staring at Vinh, who shrugged again.

Vinh looked around and located Thu, standing off to the side and watching. He waved her over and whispered to her to give these men what they needed, before walking away.

He didn't have time to deal with the politics of this mess.

If he was going to be honest, his answer to any of their questions would be simple: the Americans swam in an underground lake like idiots, and if the girl is dead, so be it. Maybe it will thwart future morons from doing the same and putting themselves in so much danger.

Instead he walked away, as if he had work to do.

"This is now our crime scene," Agent Johnson said to Vinh's back.

Vinh fought back a smile and cocked his head over his shoulder. "So… in your infinite wisdom… the poor girl is dead? Is that how we're going to play this, sir? Might as well send everyone home and get a team in to drag the water. No use in wasting any more time for a United States citizen. Right? She has been officially claimed as dead by you and your government. I'll make note of this in my report."

He now smiled when he turned and kept walking because all three agents looked annoyed and confused.

Vinh hoped Thu would deal with them now, because he was done with them. He might get into some trouble, maybe as high as a disciplinary few days off, but he didn't care. He wasn't here to play second fiddle to anyone else, especially a foreigner.

He'd dealt with American law enforcement in his past and it left a bad taste in his mouth.

Even though he'd technically been one of them.

Vinh went to the tent they'd set up and sat down in a chair, watching the DHS agents talking with Thu, who eventually walked over and stood in front of Vinh.

"You got them very angry," she said with a faint smile.

"My job is to find a missing girl, not worry about politics and people who aren't even interested in doing the right thing," Vinh said.

"What do you mean?"

Vinh wasn't going to explain himself to the woman. She was beneath him. "What are they going to do?"

"There is a large group of United States military that should be arriving very soon," Thu said. "They are planning on helping with the search. I imagine their plan is to flood the area with soldiers on land and in the lake and try to find her quickly and efficiently."

It didn't sound efficient to Vinh, but he wasn't going to tell Thu his feelings.

If they found the girl's body, so be it. He'd have less paperwork to do and it wouldn't be his fault the girl was dead. He'd been trying to find her but all of this interference had forced his hand.

Maybe I can work this in my favor, Vinh thought.

"What would you like me to do?" Thu asked.

Jump in the lake and drown, Vinh thought. "Your job is to be their shadow. Make note of anything they do. Anything they say. We need to make sure this doesn't get out of hand. You know how the United States government works."

Thu looked like she had no clue what he was talking about. Once again he'd assumed she was semi-intelligent.

"They will cut corners. Do things that aren't necessarily legal in Vietnam. Even if they somehow do a good job and find the girl alive, there will be a path of destruction in their wake. We don't mean anything to them and neither do the Vietnamese traditions. If it was up to them, they'd take over our beautiful country and use it as a military base to spread their lies and power across Asia and beyond," Vinh said.

Not that he necessarily believed everything he was saying, but there was at least a kernel of truth in his words. He knew if he was running this operation he'd have so much interference during and after it would make his head spin.

He missed the old days, before he'd even become law enforcement, when you could do your job without worry from above.

This girl is missing? Do anything and everything in your power to find her, regardless of if she's a local or a foreigner. Despite the fact she got herself into this mess, and her parents were idiots. None of that should matter because her safety used to be the only thing you worried about.

Now? If she was dead he'd have to give a hundred reasons why it had happened before he'd miraculously pulled her from the lake.

"Why are you still standing here? Go do your job," Vinh said to Thu.

Thu looked like she was about to say something but he waved his hand dismissively at her, and she turned on her heels and stomped off.

He didn't like the woman, and knew she was after his job. He also knew she would someday get it and push him out, but he wasn't too worried. He had quite a few side projects happening right now, and he knew he'd be financially fine no matter what happened.

That was the excitement of having worked in the United States and having some friends there to make money, as well as in China and here in Vietnam.

You always want several revenue streams, which I have, Vinh thought.

He knew he could likely walk away from this career right now and not miss a beat… but Vinh wasn't sure the repercussions wouldn't follow him if he did it in an unprofessional way.

His worry was simple: he'd lose face and the powers that be would make his life miserable, and his revenue streams and future would dry up. He'd be unemployed and unemployable.

Throwing it all away because he wasn't interested in his job anymore was a slippery slope he knew he was about to head down, and he didn't know how to stop it.

Not with people like Thu to deal with, let alone the DHS agents.

Vinh wondered if Thu would eventually have had enough and complained to their superiors. It had happened to him before with subordinates. He'd driven quite a few of them into other positions and at least one had quit because of him.

Was he proud of that fact? He didn't care either way. You either did your job efficiently and without getting in Vinh's way or you had to go do your below average work somewhere else. He had no time for hand-holding and trying to be a good leader or, even worse… a friend or ally.

Vinh watched as the DHS agents huddled with Thu on the shore of the underground lake.

He wanted to wander over and see what they were planning, but his pride was getting in the way as usual.

Sometimes he wished he could just go with the flow and do his job without all of these other thoughts. Constantly sizing up supposed competition, or trying to get a better angle for himself. Being selfish was tiring.

Vinh wished he'd stayed in the United States, because he could get away with more things in law enforcement. He didn't need to feel like he was constantly being watched, that his work meant something, and he was making a difference.

When was the last time in Vietnam he felt like he was doing anything important? It had been a very long time.

Vinh often counted down the days until he could properly retire, even though he was a few years off. It gave him something to strive for, a definite goal.

There was a commotion back where they'd blocked off entry to the area, and Vinh frowned when he saw a dozen or so farmed United States Marines marching toward him.

Vinh decided to actually pay attention and look like he was interested in whatever was happening.

A long line of soldiers carrying inflatable rafts was also coming now, which meant they could expand the search and find the girl's body soon enough.

Vinh wondered again what he was going to have for dinner tonight.

He strode over to Thu, who was talking to the agents.

"What's the plan?" Vinh asked, as if he hadn't previously been a jerk to these men.

If they were angry or annoyed they seemed to take it in stride.

"We're going to augment what help is already here with our military, and we've just gotten confirmation the Vietnamese military will also be arriving shortly," the lead agent said.

Thu turned to Vinh. "We should radio everyone already in the water and let them know there will be help arriving shortly."

Vinh nodded, even though he didn't need Thu to tell him what to do. "Excellent. Coordinate that." He turned to see the military already setting up the boats. "We should be able to find the girl and hopefully she'll be fine. Not too frightened. She hasn't been alone for too long. Hopefully this will be a great day for all of us."

He didn't believe she was alive. Vinh knew he'd need to stay in the front of this, though, and make sure his picture got taken when they found her. He'd need to work a few things in his head beforehand so when it was time for the press conference he would say all of the right things about the tragedy and the situation, and how everyone worked so well together.

Blah blah blah.

Vinh just needed to keep playing this game for as long as he could, and figure out how long it would take for him to get out of this awful job and this awful country.

He felt like he had way more important things to do in his life, and finding brat foreigners in places they weren't supposed to be wasn't one of them.

"Carry on," Vinh said to Thu and the agents, going back to the command tent.

CHAPTER TEN

Sally thought she felt a slight breeze on her face, a cooler wind against her tears drying on her cheeks. It was there for a second but then she stopped and couldn't find it again.

Despite spinning in a slow circle, the breeze had disappeared.

She heard the scraping of nails up ahead and knew she needed to keep following.

Why not? Without being led, even to her death, she'd eventually starve or need water.

Whatever was leading her right now had a plan but Sally didn't understand it. Was this the way out, or the way to other creatures, who would pounce on her?

There had been a dead body back there. Parts of one, anyway. Based on the fresh blood smell it hadn't been there long, which meant people were likely trying to rescue her. The tunnels could be filled with her parents and the police, but so far she hadn't heard anyone. No lights up ahead or behind, either. Sally feared the tunnel system was so vast she was miles away from the entrance she'd gone into, and no one would ever find her.

Sally thought of the body in the tunnel and knew that would eventually be her if she wasn't able to get out.

She wondered if anyone would find her body, or if it would be eaten by the denizens of the tunnels.

Her life flashed before her. She was still a teenager, still had her entire life ahead of her. She had goals and experiences ahead, and the love of her parents would be missed. Her few friends back in New York, too. She was starting to think of colleges and what she wanted to do for work and if she'd ever be married and have children. Pets, even.

So much to consider and too much to do. Dying underground was not an option.

Sally kept moving ahead, listening for the scraping noise.

There was nothing else to do right now.

She briefly wondered if she should run ahead and try to tackle or stop whatever was leading her, but the thought of touching something unknown was scarier than dying right now. What if it was a monster from her nightmares, the thing under the bed she'd been so afraid of as a child?

Her father had come in nightly to check for monsters under the bed and in the closet until she was nearly nine. Sally slept with a nightlight, even to this day.

I'm not even freaking out about the dark right now, Sally thought.

She'd just realized it. Usually she needed light around her, especially at nighttime. Or if she was in a dark place. Sally hated it when she rode the subway and it went through a tunnel and the lights flickered off, even for a second.

Now she stumbled onward, not caring what she was kicking as she moved. The ground seemed to be rising slowly up but the floor wasn't as clear of debris anymore.

Back home her friends were hanging out like usual, not worried about Sally on vacation. They often teased her because she was lucky enough to travel the world so much with her parents. Seeing exotic locales, having great stories to tell when she got back home. Meeting so many cool and interesting people.

Sally always tried to bring back little gifts for her couple of friends, too. Her father and mother encouraged it. They knew not everyone would get to travel to some of these places, and Sally wanted to share some of the fun times with her closest friends.

Her friends would wonder what had happened to her all the way in Vietnam. Especially if her body was never recovered. They'd have a memorial at the school, maybe, or a candlelight vigil for her safe return.

On the anniversary of her disappearance, her friends would get together on the rooftop and tell stories about Sally.

Years would pass and they'd all go to college and get jobs, have husbands and kids, and slowly forget about her.

Sally would be nothing after a while.

Her parents would get old and perish. Her mother might die of a broken heart, if that was a real thing. She knew her father would never forgive himself for planning this trip and the lake swim.

All it takes is one wrong move and your life is over in a second, Sally thought.

The scraping was more insistent now and she realized she'd fallen behind, too busy thinking of her destroyed future and not moving quick enough.

Afraid she'd trip over another body, Sally made her way slowly, using her good hand to feel the walls around her.

The bleeding had finally stopped on her other hand but it felt cold to the touch. She wondered if they'd need to amputate the limb.

As if you'll get out of this underground prison alive, Sally thought.

Sally struggled to keep going, her eyes feeling heavy. When was the last time she'd slept? On the plane ride to Vietnam she'd been too excited to even take a nap, staying awake and bothering her parents. Once they'd landed and checked into their hotel, the family had immediately gone out for breakfast and then right to Son Doong to swim in the underground lake.

She wished she'd been able to slow it all down and take a nap.

Not go for a swim, too.

She knew her father meant well, but he was impulsive. He liked to show off and be more of a friend than a father-figure. Sally enjoyed his company, and she knew her parents were worried as she got older Sally would stop wanting to be around them. Beg out of taking vacations each year because she had a boyfriend or a life that was more important than family.

Sally wondered if she'd ever feel like that. At fifteen, she was definitely noticing boys. There were a couple her and her friends whispered about, but none had ever asked her out on a date. None of the boys noticed her except Miguel. She didn't think she was ugly, either. Not that she thought she was a stunning beauty. She had some curves and a good personality. What more do boys want these days?

The scratching was closer than it had been. While she was dreaming about her life and boys and friends, she'd picked up the pace.

Sally ran a hand across the cold wall as she walked, careful not to miss an opening, hoping not to trip over another body.

She concentrated on the scraping noises ahead, willing herself to keep moving forward. Wanting to sleep and not worry about anything anymore.

Her eyes were so heavy and so were her limbs. Sally could barely lift her feet to walk, shuffling along on the hard surface and knowing her feet were so torn up now. Maybe she was also losing blood that way, too.

She felt cold and knew it wasn't a good thing. It was because of blood loss.

The air around her wasn't colder, it was coming from inside of her. She remembered a few things from health class, or hoped she did.

Too much blood loss was a real problem.

Sally knew she was going to die if she didn't get out of the caves and soon.

"Either kill me or help me," Sally said, her voice just above a whisper. She didn't have the strength to raise it any higher. She also meant what she said. This couldn't go on for much longer. She was too weak to keep going forward into uncertainty.

If whatever was leading her had heard or understood, it didn't stop or come back for her.

The scraping continued.

Sally closed her eyes and followed the sound.

One foot in front of the other.

If I get out of here alive I will live each day to the fullest. Isn't that what you're supposed to say? Every second will be precious and I will do my best to make the most of it all, Sally thought.

She hoped her father wasn't being too hard on himself. He hadn't forced her to go swimming. In fact, she'd thought it was a wonderful idea and had pushed to make sure they were going to do it. True, he'd figured it out a long time ago, this devious plan to swim where you weren't supposed to swim, but she'd been equally excited about it.

Her mother? Not so much. While she'd gone along with it, Sally knew her mother hated when they took risks.

"Why can't we go on vacation and simply enjoy the scenery and the food?" Her mother had said it many times in the past, but it never stopped Sally or her father from taking a risk.

Right now Sally couldn't think of a past vacation when they'd done something like this, but she knew they'd done it many times.

Her mind was getting cloudy, as if her brain was slowly shutting down. One percentage point at a time. Soon she'd have almost no thoughts that made sense in her head and her body might shut off, leaving her to die.

There was no fight or flight left in her anymore, only the cold hard fact: she was never going to get out of this alive.

Sally tried to shake her head and think clearer, but now she wasn't sure she'd only thought about thinking clearer and not actually shaken her head, or…

She wanted to cry again but had no tears left to give.

The scraping noises were getting further away.

Am I being left behind? Does the thing leading me know it's hopeless? I'm hopeless? They're going to abandon me in the tunnels. Come back for me later to feast on my cold, dead body, Sally thought.

"Wait. Please. Help me," Sally said.

Thought she said. Didn't really know if she was actually speaking or just thinking the words, trying to force herself to say them.

The scraping continued.

One bloody foot in front of the other.

CHAPTER ELEVEN

Within forty-five minutes, there were two dozen soldiers packed into half a dozen boats slowly moving across the water.

Below them were an extra dozen divers doing a sweep of the bottom of the lake, moving in tandem and keeping close together.

Not many divers had checked in yet, which was creating a problem and friction between Vinh's team and the interlopers from the United States.

Not that Vinh was too concerned. He'd washed his hands of this operation yet again, supposedly coordinating in the main tent and keeping in radio contact with the various teams.

He'd made sure to send Thu in the first boat so she had eyes and ears for their side, but mostly for Vinh.

No use in letting the girl's body be found without a Vietnamese officer at the initial scene.

Vinh had a bad feeling this was all going to play out and he'd somehow be at fault.

His phone buzzed on the table next to him, which startled Vinh. It hadn't made a sound in hours, ever since he'd climbed down into this hot, musty hole in the earth.

Checking it, he saw he had several voicemails but no signal to properly check them. Just as well because it was one of his various bosses calling to get an update.

If they're so concerned they should drive over and take a look themselves, Vinh thought.

He turned his phone off and put it into his pocket.

"Any updates?" Vinh asked the group of soldiers at another table, all crowding around a small computer monitor. He'd half-listened when they'd talked about setting up the command center with live video feeds of the search, so they could switch to various Go-Pros and cameras on their body armor.

One of the soldiers looked up for a second and shook his head. "They just started."

Vinh thought he heard another soldier chuckle and knew he'd made a comment about Vinh. Likely about the police work happening and how they'd now swoop in and make the save.

Just like all Americans. They think they rule the world, Vinh thought.

He was back to being in a bad mood. Not wanting to care about Sally or her family or his job or any of it.

Vinh needed a vacation. Not a physical one, at a beach or a fancy hotel, but a break from life. A few days to sleep in and read a book, catch up on some television programming and not have to answer to anyone.

He felt like a fool sitting by himself at another table, while the Americans ran the show.

Vinh walked over to the monitor and tapped a man on the shoulder. “Unless you’re needed to be seated this close to the action, I suggest you get up and let me sit. I’m in charge here, despite what you might think.”

The man hesitated, looking at his fellow soldiers.

“I can also arrest you for obstruction of justice. You do know what that means, right? I spent enough time working in the United States and watching your mindless police procedural shows to know they say that a lot. Too much, in fact.”

The man looked down and got out of the seat. Vinh sat and pointed at the screen.

“How many cameras can we scroll through?” Vinh asked. If he was going to have to do some work he at least needed to know some of the basics.

“Uh, twenty-two,” the man at the keyboard next to Vinh said. “I can scroll through them individually or set the computer to move from one to another in three-second intervals.”

“I don’t want to miss a thing. Is that clear? Scroll through them if you have to but I need to see every movement of every member of the tactical team," Vinh said.

He didn't want to miss anything because if they found the girl's body he wanted to make sure he knew it before anyone other than the person or persons who found it knew.

It would help him when he did his debriefing to his superiors as well as when he was front and center at the upcoming press conference, where Vinh would look solemn and not smile and talk about the tragedy that had occurred. Later, in private rooms, he'd voice his displeasure about the events to those above him and want to charge the father with his daughter's death, since he seemed to think it was no big deal to swim where they weren't supposed to swim.

Vinh would need to work on the right amount of public sorrow at the girl's loss and the push to punish the parents in private. The Vietnamese government and their police force could not and would not stand for such a slap in the face. While Vinh understood this new Vietnam was all about tourism and creating more wealth for the country, something this egregious could not go unchecked.

If it did… Vinh worried it would continue to happen. Any and every foreigner would come to this country and think they could do whatever their heart desired.

Not if Vinh could help it.

He stared at the various camera angles but all he saw was the water the boats were riding on and the darkness past the lights and not much else.

No one was talking or the sound was off.

“It seems like they are fanning out but still within sight of the team to their left and to their right,” Vinh said.

“They have strict orders not to stray too far,” the soldier said.

Vinh wanted to get up and take a walk. Do something else. This was boring so far. Find the body so they could break all of this down and move to the next part of this stupidity.

He decided to stay in his seat because he knew one of these soldiers would immediately sit down and he’d need to remind them again who was really in charge.

“Why aren’t the rest of you out there looking?” Vinh asked the assembled group crowded in the tent. “There has to be something for you to do besides stare over my shoulder.”

One or two of the soldiers mumbled and they slowly started to wander off. Vinh doubted they had assignments or actual work to do, but he didn’t like the crush of all of them so close.

“Now that we have some breathing room,” Vinh said to the man at the keyboard watching the monitor.

The man ignored the comment, switching from camera to camera but there was nothing important to see yet.

Vinh wondered how the divers were doing, too. He hadn't seen any camera shots from them yet.

"Divers seeing anything?" Vinh almost asked if they had seen the body yet. Probably not something to say out loud.

The soldier switched the screen several times until they started to see a diver making his way below the boats, faint light from above.

Under the lake was nothing but jagged rocks and swirling silt.

Vinh frowned. There wasn't any discarded trash, either. No plastic bags, no old soda cans, nothing man-made.

Until these idiot Americans fouled up the lake it had stood untouched for hundreds of years, Vinh thought. *They've ruined it. Soiled it. Gone where no man was supposed to ever have gone.*

He didn't consider himself a blind patriot of his home country, but it was aggravating to feel like Vietnam was being commercialized and Westernized and whatever other catchy phrase went along those lines. He did have some pride in where he was born and raised, even if he thought his government and the people were usually doing the wrong thing.

Vinh shook his head and tried to focus on what was happening right in front of him. There'd be times when he could pour himself a stiff drink and stare at the stars and think of all of this philosophical gunk in his head. Right now they needed to wrap all of this up so he could move on with his life.

The soldier had switched back to the feeds of the men in the boats, but there was nothing special to see on the surface of the water, either.

"This is taking too long," Vinh said. When the soldier glanced at him, Vinh had to add to what he'd said. "The poor girl could only have moments left to live. We need to find her."

The idiot thinks I'm really feeling all of that nonsense, Vinh thought.

All he could do was watch the screen as the camera flipped from one to the next, with nothing new to see except darkness and another of the boats and the soldiers in them.

He wanted to check in with Thu but didn't know why. She'd have nothing to tell him, nothing he couldn't already see.

"How big is this lake?" Vinh asked, more to himself.

The soldier grunted. "Very large. On the way over we were briefed that it can span over a mile at its widest point, and it is fairly deep in several places."

"And it was very dark until we invaded it," Vinh added sourly.

The farthest boats on either side were showing steep rock faces with nowhere to get up or use to rest. It stretched up into the ceiling and the darkness and could go for miles as well.

Vinh wondered how close to the other side they were, and if there truly was another side. Maybe the water had cut another path and that was why they couldn't find the girl. She was a few miles away, down an underground river.

Maybe there'd be falls and they'd never find her body.

"I don't see any fish," Vinh said when the soldier switched back to the diver cameras. "That seems odd."

"Maybe since nothing disturbed the lake for so long, maybe millennia, there was never anything alive down here." The soldier shrugged his shoulders as if it didn't matter to him. Only the job in front of him.

Vinh turned to see a large group of military men marching down the path toward the tent. It was the Vietnamese military. Finally.

He got up and tapped the chair. "This is my seat. Let no one else sit in it."

The soldier gave a short nod and went back to the monitor.

Vinh met with the leader of the military force, not bothering to introduce himself. "Do you have any boats? We need to get you on the water as soon as possible. The United States military is already out there but they're not finding much of anything."

"Yes, they will be arriving in a few minutes." The military man looked around at all of the people coordinating. "Is all of this necessary for one missing teenager?"

Vinh shook his head. "Not likely, but this is what we're doing. Right? We need to find the girl, not the foreigners. Understood?"

The man nodded.

"Uh, sir… you need to see this," the soldier in the tent yelled to Vinh.

CHAPTER TWELVE

Sally had lost all hope. Despite the scraping of nails up ahead in the darkness, she couldn't move another inch. She didn't remember falling, but she was sitting on the cold ground pressed up against a cold wall.

She didn't know if her eyes were open or closed. Not that it mattered. She couldn't see her hand right in front of her face if she tried.

Not that she could lift her hand to her face right now.

I just want to sleep this off and maybe I'll feel better later, Sally thought.

She closed her eyes, or thought she did.

Sleeping on the cold floor against a cold wall wasn't ideal, but it would work for Sally right now.

The scraping noise grew louder, and she thought it was only inches from her face.

"Leave me to die. I need to sleep. Go away," Sally said and swung her good arm lazily in the darkness.

Her arm connected with something hairy and she recoiled.

"Just kill me already," Sally whispered. "I can't take this anymore."

She could smell a fetid odor coming from whatever creature was inches from her. More than the smell of wet dog, it was like a wet dog that was rotting and rolling in poop. Dunked in urine, too. Disgusting.

"What are you?" Sally asked and hesitantly put out her hand again.

At first she felt nothing, but then touched the fur again. She moved her hand up and down. It was an animal covered in short, thick fur.

She didn't want to anger it or poke it in a bad place, but now she was curious. Sally knew if it was going to eat her it would've done it already.

Her hand touched what was likely a short, thick leg and down to a large furry foot with maybe three toes. Could be another one or two hidden in the thick patch of hair.

"What are you, huh?" Sally knew this was no ordinary animal, nothing she'd ever find in a book or online. Definitely not a simple species native to Vietnam.

Does Vietnam have a Bigfoot legend? Maybe this is an undiscovered creature, a cryptid beast or an alien lifeform, Sally thought.

Whatever it was, it was either helping Sally or leading her into a trap, where its family would rip her apart. She knew they were capable of it based on the body she'd stumbled upon not too long ago.

Or was it hours ago? Her head hurt. She couldn't think straight.

There were flashes of color before her eyes and she wondered if that was normal, when sight was taken from you due to absolute darkness, or if it meant she was dying because of blood loss and her organs and brain were shutting down now.

The creature seemed to move away from her. She couldn't see but she felt the movement.

Sally managed to pull herself back up against the wall and took a deep breath. She was thirsty. Hungry. So darn tired.

The scraping sound began again, only a few feet from where she was standing.

Leading her to somewhere only the creature knew.

"I'm coming. Thank you," Sally said.

At this point, even if she was being led to the slaughter, having a goal was better than being alone and unable to figure out a way to go.

Sally wished she was able to see her parents one more time and let them know how much she loved them.

How this wasn't their fault, how she'd gone along with this swim. How she was part of it and they shouldn't feel bad.

Sally started to shuffle along again, hoping her momentum would keep her upright and able to continue moving forward.

If she could just concentrate on the scraping, focus on it, let all thoughts and fears escape from her mind, and only keep heading toward the sound…

One foot in front of the other.

Sally nearly crashed head-first into a wall as she moved, her head down and eyes closed. If not for her good hand slapping the rock, she would've maybe knocked herself out or done even more damage to her body.

She idly wondered if she'd even feel it, because her body was throbbing right now. She didn't know if she was still bleeding and wasn't going to touch her bad hand and find out.

Sally remembered to raise her bad arm above her head to stop the bleeding, if it was still happening, but she couldn't tell in the dark if she was actually doing it. Her limbs were numb.

She was so cold.

The scraping noise continued. It had been an annoyance before, but now it was grating on her nerves like someone running their sharp nails down a chalkboard.

When Sally was a kid she remembered hiding behind the couch late at night while her parents watched a movie about a shark killing beachgoers, and one of the men in the movie had run his nails down a chalkboard to get everyone's attention.

Sally had groaned and her parents had found her and sent her off to bed.

For a scant second Sally thought she'd seen a light ahead and she smiled, but as she continued shuffling forward, she couldn't see it again. No matter how she tilted her head or concentrated on the darkness.

Movement was her friend. As long as she didn't feel the need to slump back down against the wall and sit on her butt, she could pretend she'd eventually be rescued or find her way out.

"Slow down, I'm fading," Sally said to the creature leading her. "You're going too fast."

The scraping sounded like it was a mile away, a faint echo, and Sally didn't know if it was because of her failing body or the creature was so far ahead now.

Another bend in the tunnel, which meant nothing to Sally. She knew they were very far away from where she'd begun her journey into the cave system.

How many miles had she walked? She didn't know. She'd run track most of her life and had good stamina under ideal conditions. If not for her injury she thought she'd still be fine.

Not that she was winded, but she was hurting. It was a definite struggle to continue. Sally tried to remember the lessons she'd learned running track about not quitting, pushing yourself for that extra burst of energy, and to never surrender to your fears or weakness.

That's all well and good, but they never taught me to persevere when you're injured and bleeding to death, while a mysterious hairy creature is leading you into a trap or to safety, Sally thought.

It would be funny if it weren't true. Sally hoped to be able to tell her friends about this someday. Maybe she'd be on the news talking about it.

She imagined her parents on either side of her, hand on her shoulder, smiles on their faces. While camera flashes snapped around her and a dozen news microphones lined up on the podium she stood behind, she'd tell her tale of courage and never giving up because she so wanted to live.

Of course she couldn't stop thinking about the news report if she was found dead of her wounds. The distraught look on her parents' faces, them holding one another and blaming themselves for this tragedy. They'd be weeping.

Sally worried her body would never be found.

Then what would happen? They'd have stock footage of the Son Doong cavern. Maybe there were police searching for her right now, too. Divers in the lake, looking for her body wedged between the rocks.

Looking for her in the wrong place.

Maybe they'd never find the tunnel she'd entered. If they did she hoped there would be markings in the dirt where she'd walked inside. She'd been placed in a cavernous room and maybe they'd find traces of her there, too.

Sally started scraping her feet against the ground, hoping there was dirt or dust and they'd be able to follow her trail.

Who were they, though? Maybe it had only been a few minutes since she'd been missing. What if her father was still in the lake, swimming, while her mother was enjoying the quiet for a few minutes? Sally had no clue how much time had truly passed.

Maybe when she'd woken up in that chamber, only seconds had passed. She'd blacked out and was only a few feet from the exit. She'd gone the wrong way and walked deeper into the cave system.

Her obvious hope was there were people searching through the caves, looking for her. Wondering if she was still alive.

Even if they were only looking for a body at this point… Sally wasn't dead. Not yet.

She kept moving along and the scraping noise grew louder. Maybe. There might just be hope she was catching up again. Or the creature was slowing down yet again so she could catch up and not get lost.

Sally tried not to think too hard on anything right now.

She knew she needed to keep going and needed to survive.

The thought of how crushing this would be to her parents was too much to bear.

As the scraping continued, Sally continued along in the darkness.

CHAPTER THIRTEEN

Vinh frowned. The soldier had called him over to show him what looked to be scuba gear piled on a rock ledge. At least two divers had dropped their items. Why?

"Search the entire area," Vinh said, as if they didn't already know to do that.

He was hoping to see a camera shot of the dead girl so they could wrap this up and go home. This was an added twist, a mystery that needed to be solved.

"Why would they leave their gear?" Vinh asked.

"Maybe they found her and she's away from the water," the soldier answered the question, thinking Vinh had asked him.

A few seconds later another camera picked up the entrance to a cave, a tunnel leading into darkness.

"Tell them to be careful," Vinh said to the soldier.

"I can't talk to them directly. Sorry. But they know what to do."

Vinh hoped so. He was worried someone else would be hurt or even killed, and he dreaded writing a thicker report about all of this. Anything wrong that happened would ultimately fall on his shoulders.

He watched as the camera went from soldier to soldier, all showing the gear and the tunnel. Over and over.

Vinh was getting a headache. “Slow down. Find whoever is in the lead and working toward the opening and focus on that camera for now.”

The soldier complied, and Vinh sighed in relief. He was sure this soldier was raised on videogames like the rest of his generation, and the fast shots and changing views were no big deal to him, but to Vinh it was annoying.

Vinh smiled when he saw Thu was right behind the lead soldier, only a step behind. She seemed fearless and if she wasn’t so cloying and wanting his job, Vinh thought he might have been friendly with her. Not friends. He never truly associated with his colleagues if he could help it. Never went out for a beer after their shift, never talked about personal things with anyone.

His private affairs were his private affairs, and he couldn’t care less about their personal lives, either.

Especially about Thu. He had unbridled contempt for the woman. She was so quick to inject herself in any investigation she thought could get her ahead, to make her look good. He wondered if she’d been assigned to this case or if she'd volunteered. He wouldn't put it past her to have shown up unannounced, offering her help.

Of course, she knew better than to do that with Vinh. He would've sent her home and added it in his report. His superiors knew he didn't like working with her, and Vinh also knew she'd complained a couple of times about the way he talked to her.

Vinh had made sure never to say anything inappropriate. Nothing that could come back and haunt him.

But he made it clear he didn't want her around, didn't respect her and would never see her as an equal. He'd never addressed his issues with his superiors. He didn't think he needed to. They knew he wasn't a fan of her or her style of investigating, and she was the one with a couple of blemishes on her record. Not Vinh.

He knew he'd messed up quite a few cases over the years, but he was smart enough to cover his own tracks. Put the blame on someone or something else. He wasn't above planting evidence if it meant taking a bad person off of the street, either.

Vinh knew what his job was: to rid the world of bad people. He did it whichever way he needed to do it. The means justify the ends. He slept well at night knowing he always did the right thing for the greater good.

Thu was a glory hound, and she seemed to enjoy the spotlight. Vinh was sure she'd try to get close to the podium when this was all over, either smiling brightly if the girl was actually found, or looking somber with her head bowed if the body was recovered.

Either way, the woman was going to try to be within camera range.

Vinh would need to make note in his report, as subtly as possible so as not to draw attention back on himself, about the missteps Thu had made so far today. Failure to move swiftly when necessary, not calling in the military fast enough… all he'd need was a couple of things to point out.

Orders he'd either given her or she should've already known to do. He'd 'blame' himself for not following up with Thu, assuming she'd been doing this long enough to know the protocol and the steps that needed to be followed and how quickly they'd need to be implemented.

Thu might finally be out of his hair, and he'd quietly rejoice.

Vinh's radio crackled but it was only static.

He could see on the screen Thu was trying to contact him.

"Can you tune that in better?" Vinh asked.

The soldier shook his head. "They're in a dead zone. I'm surprised we got that much, to be honest. I have no radio contact with any of them, even if we needed to message. They're on their own."

"Then I hope they know what they're doing," Vinh said. "This is being recorded, right?"

"Yes, sir."

Vinh hoped Thu would screw up and make a huge mistake. Even if it cost the life of one of the soldiers, it would be worth it to Vinh.

Of course, if something bad happened to her it would be even better.

Vinh didn't believe he was an awful person, but he knew he was never going to be a kind or forgiving one, either. Everyone had a place in this world, and his place was to be on top. A predator and never the prey, like Thu.

Like this stupid soldier watching the monitors.

"What are they doing?" Vinh asked. The view kept going in and out, a few lines of static on the monitors increasing with each second.

"I told you… they are in a bad spot right now. It's hard to get a good signal. I'm doing the best I can, but without better equipment, it is what it is," the soldier said.

Vinh wondered if this man was being rude or just trying to explain the predicament they were currently in. He decided to give the man a break. For now.

"We need to figure out what they're currently seeing," Vinh said. He pointed at the monitor. "Like… what is that right there?"

The soldier sighed. "It looks like a cave mouth. They've found a natural opening in the rocks. Might be the only way to see it from the ledge, too. I'm guessing if you were in the lake, even on a boat, you'd never be able to see it from that angle."

Vinh wondered why divers had dropped their gear, but he knew they'd gone into the cave mouth. What was through that entrance, and where were the divers now?

"We might have more than a teenage girl missing at this point," Vinh said.

He thought of all the paperwork he'd have to do tonight. Maybe it would be better for Thu to survive this, long enough to do her share of the writing, and then he'd bury her in his own report.

"Why aren't they going into the entrance?" Vinh asked.

The soldiers were all lined up and looked ready to go, but Thu was talking to them. The sound was cutting in and out and Vinh couldn't hear a word she was saying, but he assumed she was giving them some rah-rah pep talk, as if these hardened warriors needed some skinny little Vietnamese woman to explain how things in the real world worked.

"Let them go already," Vinh said through gritted teeth.

He hated her more and more with each passing moment.

Thu was still talking, pointing at the cave mouth and then the lake and then… "Where is she pointing at? Get in there and find the girl already," Vinh shouted.

He noticed a few of the soldiers in the area, attempting to look busy, gave him a sideways look. He wanted to shout at them now, tell them to do something useful. Two dozen men and women with nothing else to do but stand around. This was how the government worked and how the taxpayer's money was being spent.

Vinh decided not to go into a diatribe about any of that, knowing his own personal feelings. Right now… he wanted Thu to get out of the way or lead the charge into the unknown.

All of this was definitely going into his report.

"You're sure this is being taped, right? Will it have the sound in the recording, though?" Vinh really wanted to hear what stupidity Thu was spewing to these soldiers.

"What we can hear is what is being recorded," the soldier said and shrugged. "So… no. Only the video will be available, I'm afraid."

Vinh hoped it was good enough. With luck, the idiot teenage girl was only a few feet inside the cave, likely scared and paralyzed with fear.

They'd extract her quickly and Vinh could call it in and begin wrapping all of this mess up.

He wondered how much business had been lost since this started. Perhaps the stupid Americans would have to pay for the lost money and wages of the people who worked at Son Doong.

"She's done with her speech," the soldier said. Even he had an edge to his words. He knew she should've stepped aside and let them do their job.

Vinh smiled when two soldiers stepped in front of Thu and entered the entrance to the cave, their lights shining into the darkness.

CHAPTER FOURTEEN

Thu knew she couldn't go first, but she was happy to be third into the cave.

There was a weird glowing fungus on the walls but it looked smeared and didn't extend too far inside.

Had Sally done it, or one of the divers? Had they touched it? What if it was poisonous or deadly? I'll need to come back for a sample after we find them, Thu thought.

She was in love with law enforcement but she dabbled in other things, all to make herself better. Thu had several degrees that had nothing to do with her job, things she studied and enjoyed.

Botany, various sciences, she was writing a nonfiction book about her grandfather's life before, during and after the Vietnam War and what it had done to him, and a fiction book about an awful police chief that did a bad job and made the team below him dislike all of his policies and rules.

Thu was definitely writing this book about her treatment from Vinh, who she detested. Despite not wanting to work with him, and knowing the man would blame her for every single thing that went wrong, Thu needed to maintain her composure and cover herself by documenting everything said between them.

She'd been recording every conversation they'd had in the past few months since no one above them believed her, or they did but didn't want to rock the boat. Vinh was an accomplished officer who'd been in law enforcement in the United States, and he could smile when he needed to and he definitely played the political game to get ahead and to push everyone else down.

Thu didn't want to bury Vinh. Her goal was to keep her job, move up and gain more power and pay, and keep studying the things in life she was interested in. She had no time for dating or boring hobbies. She only owned a television so she could watch videos of those things that she was interested in studying.

But if Vinh kept up with the shenanigans and not playing fair, Thu knew she'd have no choice but to call him on it. In public. She'd release some of the choice bits from her tapes, which she'd collected into specific files on her computer. Hundreds of hours.

Hundreds of quotes from Vinh, all condescending and embarrassing for a man who thought he always controlled the narrative.

Thu knew when the time finally came for her to retire, she might release them at that point. As long as Vinh was still alive to enjoy the blowback from all of it, of course.

She doubted he'd play nice until then, and she'd be releasing them sooner than later. Especially if he somehow got her fired or reprimanded. If her superiors weren't willing to back her, she'd make sure the public did it.

It would be another blow to the police in Vietnam, but she wouldn't be the cause of it. She'd be the whistleblower who exposed the ugly truth.

Thu didn't want revenge, she wasn't trying to ruin anyone's career. She was trying to hold onto her own and retire in peace. After doing a good job with many accolades and successful cases closed in her career.

The soldiers were moving now, and she was swept up in the tide. Thu wished she had something more than her standard-issue weapon, but didn't think there'd be a gun battle.

More than likely they'd find the girl with a couple of divers, all of them lost and trying to escape the maze of tunnels they might encounter.

There were so many headlights shining up and down and left to right, Thu thought she'd get dizzy. Add in the fast pace they were moving and she knew she'd get a headache and maybe be sick by the time this was over.

To these soldiers, this was business as usual. A tactical formation, an unknown threat ahead of them, and they knew exactly what to do.

After a hundred feet or so they came to a fork in the tunnels and without a word they were rushing equally in both directions, Thu being swept to the right.

At times she felt like she wasn't even walking or running, simply being carried in the tight grouping.

She could smell the aftershave of the man behind her, he was so close, his rifle aimed over her shoulder at times as they moved. Thu worried if they engaged in a firefight the sound of the weapon so close to her head might rupture her eardrum.

Not that anything like that will happen, Thu thought. *This is a rescue mission, not a war exercise*.

She really hoped it wasn't a war exercise. While she wasn't afraid of guns, she'd owned one since the day she legally could, a fight in these close spaces would be loud and obnoxious.

The tunnel split again and so did the soldiers in equal measure. She decided to keep going to the right.

While it was uneven in places, these tunnels looked hand-carved. Man-made? She didn't think anyone had been down here. Ever. Son Doong hadn't been discovered that long ago.

Maybe they were traveling through the same passages ancient civilizations of Vietnam had traversed. The thought of it was humbling.

Thu would need to follow up in the future and try to explore this with a group. The idea there could be so much archeological evidence so close was amazing to her.

I could discover an ancient, unknown piece of our history, Thu thought.

She wished they weren't moving so fast, because she would love to stop for a couple of minutes and examine the walls and floors and ceiling closer. There might be artifacts.

At the next larger cavern, maybe three times as wide as the tunnel, Thu shifted as far to her right as she could and managed to get out of the stream of men. There weren't a lot of them left now that they'd split a couple of times, but enough she was growing impatient before they were all past her.

Now, to see what I can see, Thu thought.

She used her light to shine it on the walls and was startled to see so many claw marks cut into the rocks at about waist-level. There were lines that went left to right as far as she could see, and marks on the floor as well.

Nothing higher than maybe her chest, and those marks seemed much rarer.

What is making all of these marks? There is an animal or animals down here, and they have sharp claws, Thu thought.

She hoped the sheer number of soldiers would scare them off and the animals would find hiding places until they'd found the girl and the divers. Now she worried something had happened to them, and they'd been attacked.

Thu tried to use her radio to get Vinh and let him know what she'd found. Not because she felt like she needed to check in with him, but because she was trying to cover her own butt. She didn't want him to use anything against her, and telling him what was happening as it happened was a good thing.

She got only static when she tried. Giving up, she turned the radio off and clipped it back onto her belt.

Her light didn't find anything else but the claw marks. She had no clue how big the animal would be that made them, but it seemed like it wouldn't be that big if it was only a meter or two off of the ground.

If the creature was walking on four legs, it might mean it was as large as a small bear.

Maybe. Thu wished she had a camera with her. She had left her phone and personal items behind, fearing they'd get wet. That was a stupid thing to do, she now knew.

A few pictures of the scratches would be good for future reference.

Thu hoped she didn't come face to face with whatever had created the scratches. She wondered what type of animal lived down here in the dark. Was there a way for them to get out, to see the sun and feel the breeze? Or was it an underground beast that had never seen the light of day? The idea was interesting. Maybe they were on the cusp of finding a new animal, hidden for untold generations inside the bowels of Son Doong.

She walked slowly in the direction the soldiers had moved, casting her light on the walls and light and trying to see if there was anything else she could find.

A dozen steps more and the light glinted on something white on the ground. Thu bent and smiled.

It was a large canine tooth, thick at its base and pointed at the top. Thu picked it up gingerly and put it in her hand, frowning.

The tooth was bigger than a human tooth, and she could see part of the bottom had been cracked. Likely the reason the tooth was no longer in a mouth.

But a mouth of what? Thu had no real knowledge of teeth, but now she wanted to know more. She decided to pocket the tooth and find a knowledgeable experienced person to give her better insight.

If I get out of this. I might be lost, Thu thought.

She decided she'd dawdled behind enough and needed to catch up with the men with weapons in hand. Especially if there was an animal in these caves with very large, sharp teeth.

Thu hoped she could find the path the soldiers had been heading.

Not that she needed it, because she heard the first scream up ahead, not too far off.

CHAPTER FIFTEEN

It was utter chaos only a few turns down a tunnel.

A soldier had fallen, his throat slashed, and his light on his helmet was pointing at the low ceiling, casting shadows.

Another light was bobbing up and down as Thu approached. The soldier was crawling toward her, and the light kept shining right into her eyes. She saw stars, trying to blink it away.

Thu turned away but bumped into someone as they ran past her, screaming.

She'd never heard such a blood-curdling yell in her life, and so close.

Thu fell to her knees and covered her head, not knowing what was happening but knowing it wasn't good.

There was gunfire up ahead. Several short bursts of an automatic weapon.

When her eyes finally adjusted back, she saw three men had been killed.

On closer inspection of the nearest one, Thu was horrified to see his throat had been slit open as if by a claw.

Like the claw marks on the walls.

Thu picked up one of the automatic weapons on the ground, fearful her own service weapon wouldn't have enough firepower against whatever was attacking them.

She took a few steps forward, keeping her light moving back and forth.

When she got to the next intersection, seeing the split left and right, she stopped and listened.

In both directions came the distant sounds of gunfire and screams.

Thu went to the right and a few paces in she stopped.

On the ground, dead and riddled with bullet holes, was a small furry creature. White, sightless eyes, overlarge teeth and nails, and an elongated snout like a wolf.

There were more claw marks on the walls.

She tried her radio again but all she got was static. Thu hoped the live feed was still connected and Vinh and the others were seeing what was happening ahead.

Thu wished she knew what was happening ahead, too.

Maybe I should turn back and get more help, she thought.

If Vinh saw her running away he'd have a field day with it. He'd accuse her of abandoning the soldiers, the missing girl, and her job. She'd be raked through the coals on this one, and she'd burn her career to the ground.

No, she needed to figure out what was happening. Obviously they'd been attacked. Maybe ambushed by the small menacing monsters.

What were they? Thu had definitely never seen anything like it. A wolf hybrid, perhaps? Maybe a creature that had survived for hundreds or thousands of years in isolation underground.

Their eyes didn't seem to work, not as white as they were. Which made sense since there was no light down here.

Forcing herself to keep going, Thu made sure not to miss anything as she moved. She was able to collect several clips for the weapon either loose on the ground or from the pockets of the next two fallen soldiers in the tunnel.

Not that she hoped to have to shoot at the animals that were attacking the soldiers. She hoped by the time she caught up the brief skirmishes would be over.

Another minute of walking and she saw another fallen soldier, his legs and arms sliced up. She smelled the blood and gagged. Based on the stench ahead as she proceeded, she knew what she was going to find.

A soldier had been eviscerated, his intestines spilled across the ground in all directions.

Thu had to walk through the gore and she felt bile rising in her throat. She threw up some of the coffee she'd had a few hours ago. Careful not to slip and fall and cover herself in blood, Thu made sure to have one hand on a wall at all times.

There were more gunshots ahead.

She was trying not to panic. Her meager light was casting shadows on the walls, making it hard to not panic. Every step forward and she thought she was under attack, but it was only the darkness trying to get to her.

Thu kept moving and ignored the next couple of dead soldiers in her path. At a large natural crossroads, where three tunnels connected, she saw another couple of bodies.

Everyone was ripped apart, their legs bent at obscene angles and their bodies mangled.

She scooped up some more clips for the weapon in her hand, hoping she didn't need to use it.

How many soldiers had come over? Maybe they're all dead, Thu thought.

She might be able to find her way back but wondered how many turns she'd taken. It was a maze. While the tunnels seemed relatively flat in spots, they dipped up and down at times. She had no idea how high or low she was compared to the original entrance. Or where it was, exactly.

Knowing she needed to keep moving forward and find out if any of the soldiers were still alive, she took a deep breath and tried her best to remain calm.

I've been in tense situations before, Thu reminded herself. She'd been involved in a few arrests that had gone wrong, with suspects shooting at the police. She'd been manhandled by suspects a number of times as well, because they only saw her as a petite woman. Her martial arts training had come in handy in those times.

She had the scrapes and bruises to show for all of her work over the years, too.

I'm not going to let a jerk like Vinh run me off of the police force, Thu thought.

Another deep breath and Thu was off, moving faster now. Nearly in a jog, trying to locate survivors and face the creatures living here. She knew she couldn't hesitate. Couldn't waste a second overthinking any of this.

The time had come for action, and she focused on that. Tried to relax and change her mindset to the task at hand, which was fighting against this foe and getting out alive.

There was more gunfire echoing but it was hard to tell where it was coming from. Behind her or in front of her? Maybe in another tunnel somewhere else. It was so hard to gauge the sound.

Thu kept moving forward, calmer since she had a loaded weapon at her disposal. If nothing else, she should be able to fight her way out of this.

More body parts and blood down the tunnel.

What if I can't fight them off? These are trained soldiers and they're being ripped apart. What chance do I have? Not a very good one, Thu thought.

She kept moving forward, hoping to find an exit or the living soldiers.

The hope was there were still some alive.

Thu wished she'd had a camera mounted on her head like the others. Maybe Vinh and whoever was watching would see what she was seeing, which was a lot of dead people as well as whatever it was they were fighting.

What exactly was attacking them? Thu couldn't figure it out, even seeing them up close. Furry beasts, tiny monsters? They were like the stuff of nightmares.

Fangs and claws. Like killing machines. How long had they been down here, an unknown animal? She wondered if the teenage girl who'd gone missing or the divers looking for her had somehow disturbed them.

Maybe it was her and the soldiers who'd stumbled into their lair and they were merely defending their territory.

Were they intelligent or just mindless creatures, only caring about eating and fighting?

Thu had so many questions. Despite the danger she was in, it was still exhilarating. Maybe she'd be the lone survivor and could tell her story to the news agencies. Become a media star. The woman who fought off these monsters and lived to tell the story. For a price, of course.

Then she wouldn't have to worry about Vinh and his backstabbing. She could make real money and get her fifteen minutes of fame and hope to bank enough to live off of it for the rest of her life.

She just needed to survive.

At the next fork in the tunnel there was more blood and another dead creature. She realized she hadn't heard gunshots in over a minute, which was either a good sign or a bad one.

Maybe they've cleared out the monsters and it's safe up ahead, Thu thought.

A few steps later she heard the distant echo of more gunfire and knew they weren't out of the woods yet.

She heard a scraping noise behind her and Thu turned in time to see three of the creatures a few meters behind, watching her as they approached.

Thu started to fire, cutting down the monsters as they rushed to take her down, dropping them to the ground.

She fired a few more rounds into them to make sure they were truly dead.

The tunnel was smokey and the stench of the ripped apart bodies made her vomit.

Had she heard more scraping sounds behind her now, as she'd turned? Thu swung back the way she was headed and looked.

The tunnel up ahead was empty.

Don't let your mind play tricks on you now. You might be so close to surviving, Thu thought.

She had to keep moving. There might be danger behind and danger ahead, but Thu knew she needed to face it. Face not only her fears but survive.

Thu reminded herself she had a story to tell, a very rich and wonderful one. If she could get out of this with her life.

Ahead were more gunshots, long bursts.

Maybe a final battle was occurring.

Thu didn't want to miss anything, because she wanted more for her story. More to talk about during interviews.

More and more. Thu was going to blow this all wide open.

If only she could survive.

CHAPTER SIXTEEN

Thu saw lights swirling up ahead but she didn't want to rush headlong into danger, so she took her time. The gunfire was ringing out occasionally now, and she knew at least one or two soldiers were still alive.

She kept looking back, sure a creature was going to sneak up on her and slice her hamstring or stab her in the back.

Only darkness followed her down the tunnel.

Thu followed the curve of the tunnel to her right, where the light was coming from. It seemed dimmer now, or maybe not as much light as when she'd first seen it.

Maybe the creatures are killing the soldiers and dousing the lights, she thought.

She was right. As she entered a large natural chamber, she saw only three soldiers were still alive, backs to one another, firing at dozens of the creatures pressing at them.

The monsters were stepping on and crushing the head lamps and torches, slowly plunging the cavern into darkness.

Thu needed to join the fight, and she knew the soldiers had their cameras still working, so anyone watching the live feed would see her, too. The last thing Thu needed was to be caught paralyzed with fear and not helping.

She opened fire at a group of the creatures not engaged in the battle yet, standing off to the side as if waiting for an opening to pounce.

The automatic weapon cut them to ribbons in seconds.

Several of the creatures turned toward Thu, realizing they had yet another foe in their midst.

Thu swung the weapon around at them but it was either jammed or she was out of ammo.

Groaning, Thu checked the weapon, saw she had no more ammo, and slammed another clip into the weapon.

The creatures were still a couple of meters away, and she mowed them down quickly.

They die within a few rounds, so why is everyone being killed? This makes no sense, she thought.

As she was searching for another target, one far enough away from the soldiers so she didn't risk hitting them with friendly fire, she saw what was happening.

The creatures were dropping from the darkness above, crashing down on the soldiers and driving them to the ground. As soon as a soldier went down, there was a rush from those around to attack and keep the man down.

Within a couple of minutes, all three remaining soldiers had been pummeled, death from above. They were ripped apart.

Thu backed away slowly, nearly tripping over another dead soldier. She kept her eyes on the monsters as they feasted on the corpses, reaching down and picking up whatever weapons and ammo she could find.

She also grabbed one of the camera headbands, hoping it was still working. She ignored the blood on it and strapped it to her head, just above her own light. Better to have more light than none, and if one of the lights was destroyed in an attack, she might still be able to see.

The thought of total darkness without light was frightening to Thu.

Counting at least twenty of the creatures left, and one eye to the darkness above, Thu needed to get out of the cavern so they couldn't get above her. She backed slowly into the tighter tunnel, pacing a couple of meters back.

Careful she didn't trip on anything and nothing was sneaking up behind her, Thu pressed against a wall and watched as the creatures gathered in the cavern. Dozens of them.

"If you can hear me out there… send more soldiers, but let them know to shoot on sight. These monsters are dangerous. They'll swarm you, they'll drop from the ceiling, they have sharp claws and fangs. They are truly dangerous, and I'm not sure if anyone else is even alive at this point," Thu said, hoping someone could hear her.

Hoping Vinh was listening, and saw how heroic she was being. She doubted he would last more than a few minutes against these creatures and against these odds.

Thu planted her feet and made sure the extra clips were in her pocket and within reach. She hoped she had enough ammo to battle every last one of them, and knew even if Vinh got this message in real time, it would take nearly an hour for more soldiers to find more boats and row across the big lake, find the entrance and then the right tunnel to find her.

By then she was certain it would be too late.

Three monsters crossed the imaginary line Thu had set in the tunnel and she opened fire, killing them. What was left of their small bodies hit the ground, and she nearly vomited when the smell of their mangy fur and open bodies hit her. Now she worried she'd pass out from the noxious gasses and awful stench.

Another two creatures appeared but they didn't cross the line. Instead, they grabbed what was left of their kind and dragged them back into the chamber.

Maybe they'll eat their dead and leave me alone for a few minutes, Thu thought.

She turned her head when she thought she heard a scraping noise in the distance, but now she wondered if it was just the echo of so many monsters in the cavern, playing tricks on her mind.

Thu knew if she tried to escape the creatures would be at her back, and they seemed to be very fast and agile.

Again, she wondered what they were? A lost race of creatures, hidden for hundreds or thousands of years? If she could figure out a way to knock one of them out, maybe this would be the greatest discovery in decades.

Not that she'd try to get that close to them. The smell alone might kill her, let alone tooth and claw.

Thu glanced away again, wondering when her fight or flight was going to kick in. She couldn't stand here dumbly while the creatures figured out a new way to get to her.

Even now, they might be circling behind her to cut off her escape. They would certainly know every last inch of their underground home.

Thu didn't know whether to stay or go. If she started to run back, hoping she could find her way, they might get behind and drag her down. She might also run right into a group of them, lying in wait to ambush her.

Though, if she stayed where she was, she knew eventually she'd run out of ammo.

A creature rushed into the tunnel at her, and Thu shot it down, trying not to waste ammo. Two or three shots would drop them.

It was close enough to the mouth of the tunnel two creatures tried to grab the remains, but Thu took a step forward and killed them, too. Her goal was to wipe them out.

Kill or be killed.

She was sweating, so much her hands were slick. Her face was a mask of sweat and she worried it would drip from her hair and blind her. Even for a couple of seconds, while she was wiping her eyes, the creatures could get a jump on her.

Five more monsters burst into the tunnel. Thu took a deep breath and let them come so it would be harder for their fellow creatures to extract them.

Already she could see a number of them behind this attack group going for their dead.

Thu opened fire, trying to not only kill the initial five but the others before they carried the bodies off.

She managed to kill all but one of them, who dragged two bodies out and disappeared into the cavern.

Another noise behind her made Thu turn, but there was nothing there.

Or maybe it was in the distance. Could it be soldiers coming to rescue her? Maybe Vinh had seen the attacks from the beginning and had sent in another group to wipe out the creatures.

He'd likely try to toss every man, woman and child with a gun into the tunnels to destroy these things and be the hero, she thought.

Thu hoped whatever she was seeing via the camera was being filmed, so she had proof she'd been the one underground fighting for her life, while Vinh sat on his butt and watched.

Deciding to stay was to die, Thu started to walk slowly backward, making sure not to trip over a body or get ambushed. It was slow-going and she worried she'd take a wrong turn at some point and end up in a tunnel that was a dead end or took her further into the unknown.

"If you can hear me, I need help. Now," Thu said. "Just follow the blood and the bodies."

She came to a fork in the tunnel she didn't remember, wondering if she'd already gone the wrong way.

Three creatures appeared from the other tunnel and she shot them down, waiting for the smoke to clear and to see or hear if there were more of them.

A noise behind her turned Thu around, in time to see a large group of creatures rushing at her. She opened fire and didn't let off the trigger until she was sure they were all dead.

Could there be hundreds of them? Would I run out of ammo soon enough and be swarmed? I need to save as much ammo as I can, Thu thought.

It was hard to keep track of the shots when the monsters were after her, and she was always on the verge of panic. She knew no manner of therapy was ever going to get her past this. She thought she'd likely need to sleep with the light on and her weapon nearby for the rest of her life.

As long as she lived.

They were definitely following her now as she moved.

She heard the scraping of nails on the walls behind her but she couldn't be sure if she was able to keep them at a distance or if they were going to catch up to her.

Aware of her surroundings, she made sure to shine the light above her head when she entered parts of the tunnel that had a higher ceiling. It saved her life at least twice, when she looked up to see a creature or two clinging to the darkness above, waiting for her to pass underneath them.

Thu shot the creatures, trying not to get hit by their falling bodies. She was covered in blood and gore now, though.

She paused to wipe the blood from her head light and the camera, hoping what she was dealing with was still being broadcast.

More scraping from behind and it definitely sounded closer now.

Thu was tired. She was hot and sweaty, the air stifling and smelled like coppery blood.

At least these things bleed and die, she thought.

Thu knew she hadn't come this way before when she stepped into a large cavern, where she saw dugouts in the rocks all around. There was what looked like dried grass and plants stuffed into the cutouts. This was their home, where they slept.

A small pile of human and fish bones were in the middle of the room, and there were also groupings of other items spaced apart: old scuba gear, spears and rifle parts, moldy clothing, a stack of leather shoes and what might be pieces of automobiles or planes.

Thu lifted her head slowly and saw a dozen of the creatures on higher shelves, ready to pounce.

She opened fire, killing them as they dropped down.

From behind her she heard the scraping and turned, finger on the trigger. As more of the creatures rushed into the main area, Thu made sure to keep them from spreading out and getting too close. She kept an eye above in case there were more there, too.

Her clip was emptied but she slammed in the next one and then the next.

There were dozens of creatures. Based on the amount of sleeping areas in this chamber, and assuming this was the only one, there could be upwards of a hundred of them.

Thu kept firing until she was out. Her weapon was hot to the touch and she knew she'd have burns on her hands and arms.

She checked her pockets for another clip but there was none. She'd spent them all.

Maybe fifteen of the creatures were still alive, and they surrounded her.

"Come on. Let's finish this," Thu screamed, now using the rifle as a club. She wished she'd had time to go through the piles for a more suitable weapon.

Then gunfire burst all around her and she fell to the ground. Had one of the monsters learned how to shoot a weapon?

No. Dozens of soldiers entered the cavern from the various exits, cutting down the creatures as they swarmed inside.

Thu sighed and stood with a smile.

"Spread out and make sure there are none left," one of the soldiers barked. He turned to Thu and smiled. "We came as soon as we could. We were watching from a remote feed. Ma'am, you are my hero."

CHAPTER SEVENTEEN

This was Vinh's worst-case scenario, happening right before his eyes. What scared him the most was he realized he was rooting for the monsters to kill Thu so he didn't have to be pushed aside.

She seemed unstoppable. She was killing them at every turn, even though the odds were firmly against her.

Vinh had wanted to hold off on sending more soldiers to help her, hoping a delay, even by a few minutes, would prevent her from escaping.

I want her dead. I am a really bad person, Vinh thought.

He'd been able to watch her feed and at the same time watch the new batch of soldiers, all heavily-armed, rush into the tunnels and kill anything that moved. They knew what they were dealing with, and this second wave of men and women had direct communication with the military, which had now taken over this mission.

Vinh had been relegated to standing on his toes and looking over the military men conducting the extract.

"We still need to find the teenager," the soldier at the screen was saying. "And make sure this tough woman gets help, before it's too late."

Vinh knew if Thu fell, she'd be praised forever. A martyr for the cause. He worried the public would wonder why she'd been sent into danger, while he was standing in a crowded tent watching everything unfold, a cup of coffee in his hand.

I need to go over every scenario in my head, Vinh thought.

If she survived he'd openly praise her, letting her know what a hero she was. Thu would need to be put high on a pedestal, even though it might cost Vinh his job eventually. If she got out of this alive, and continued to kill so many creatures… she'd be a national hero.

Dozens of soldiers had fallen because of the monsters, and yet Thu had single-handedly cleared a path for herself.

Vinh wanted to walk away from all of this but knew it would be in poor form. Once the smoke had cleared, especially if she'd survived, there would be a lot of questions. If he wasn't nearby, watching like everyone else, he'd be in deep, deep trouble.

Even if Thu fell and was slain, there'd be too many questions. Vinh wondered if his career had come to a close.

Why did I let her go with the soldiers? I should've had her here, at my side, so she couldn't affect the outcome of any of this, Vinh thought. Too late.

Vinh moved to the side to get a better look. There were multiple camera angles and the soldier at the controls kept switching through them. Nothing but dead creatures in every shot.

Groups of the military had spread out and he saw a couple of them were hand-drawing a rudimentary map of the tunnels.

"We need to make sure there isn't an area we haven't explored," someone was saying. "I want it all figured out by the time we pull out. Has the body of the girl been found yet?"

Vinh got excited, thinking he meant the body of Thu. Had she been killed? Either by a creature or friendly fire?

No. She was alive and smiling. Being led by three soldiers out of the tunnels and into one of the many boats in the lake.

Thu was on her way back, where she'd be praised for a job well-done.

Was it, though? She hadn't found the girl, Vinh thought. The job was simple: to find the teenager. He didn't see she'd been found. Maybe that was something he could focus on if it came to his head on the chopping block.

Vinh tried to push to the front but he was shouldered out by much bigger men, who gave him frowns but didn't say a word to him.

He realized this command was no longer his at all. He wasn't even in a secondary role now, the military having taken over.

"She's coming out. She should be landing back here in twenty."

Vinh decided to walk down to the shoreline and wait for Thu. He'd be the first to greet her with a smile and a handshake. Hopefully someone would be there with a camera. Maybe he could get a good photo opportunity out of this. He'd tell his boss he'd sent her in because he knew she could handle it. Thu was under his command, after all, and he'd been her mentor.

There was no way Vinh was going to look bad in this situation.

Maybe the soldiers still clearing the tunnels would eventually find the dead teenage girl, and Vinh could look at her parents and shake his head. He'd still say the right things to them, the words they needed to hear, but what he wanted to say he'd never be able to say without killing his career.

He could see the boat approaching and he planted his feet and rolled his shoulders. He put on his biggest smile, trying to look calm.

Trying to look like all of this was planned and had gone even better than expected. No surprises, because he had all the faith in the world in Thu and what she could do.

Maybe, with any luck, she'd be promoted out of his unit and into a tactical one in another building. In another city. Vinh could still attach himself to her great showing today, and subtly say he'd trained her for combat and handling pressure under intense fire.

If he'd had more time Vinh would've let the media in so they could get the pictures and the story – according to him – and get it in the paper. Of course, if anyone mentioned the missing girl he'd defer to Thu since her mission going with the soldiers was to find her.

Once the media realized she might have shown her skills as a killer of small hairy creatures, but she couldn't rescue the girl… Vinh kept smiling, savoring the taste of his imminent victory in all of this.

The boat landed and a couple of soldiers helped Thu out of the boat. She still had the automatic weapon slung over her shoulder and she was covered in blood.

What was that American movie he'd seen years ago? Rambo? Something like that. Thu looked like a female version of the lead actor in her current state.

Now he was glad he hadn't brought the media in yet. She looked like a warrior, covered in the blood of her enemy. A sight that would be on the cover of every newspaper come morning.

Vinh looked up at the ceiling, wondering if it was night yet. He'd lost all track of time being underground. Not that it mattered. He was going to sleep well whenever he got home.

Thu was approaching him at a fast pace.

Vinh held out his hand to shake and hopefully get someone to take the picture, because now the soldiers in the tent were flooding out to see her.

"Job well–"

Thu took Vinh's hand and squeezed it. Hard. She was smiling but leaned in close, cutting him off. "I'm going to get your job. Be prepared. You screwed up."

Vinh's smile faltered.

"I have recorded every conversation we've ever had, and the bosses know about it," Thu said. She was still gripping his hand and Vinh tried in vain to pull away from her. He was sweating. People were now surrounding them.

"If I were you, I'd leave now and clean out your desk. There won't be a job to come back to tomorrow." Thu smiled. "I can't wait to have the biggest and best party when you're gone. Everyone, and I mean everyone, will be happy. Except for you. I imagine you'll be relegated to a traffic cop position. Writing tickets in some out of the way village until you can retire with a pension, although it will be less since they'll likely bust you down a few ranks, too."

Thu released his hand and walked toward the crowd waiting for her.

Everyone cheered and Thu waved them off. "I'm no hero. The men and women who died in those tunnels are the heroes. They need to be remembered. We haven't found the teenager yet, but I'm told we have tracks for her. She might even still be alive. Wouldn't that be great?"

Thu glanced back at Vinh and winked, as if he was on her side and they were sharing a moment.

The last true moment of my career, Vinh thought. At this point he could hope to still have a job as a meter worker somewhere off the grid. Instead, he had a feeling he'd be dragged through the coals and tossed out in a very big public showing.

If the bosses had let her tape every conversation, that meant Vinh was in trouble. He'd ridiculed her, talked down to her, and had threatened her job on more than one occasion.

Right now, as he watched Thu shine in the spotlight on her, Vinh knew he'd hardly ever said a positive word to the woman.

It was all coming back to haunt him.

With nothing else left for him to do and not wanting to see everyone patting Thu on her back, Vinh walked out of Son Doong and toward his police cruiser.

Past the news media in the parking lot.

His phone was ringing and he saw he'd received several messages already.

Vinh answered on the second ring and held his breath. It was his superior officer.

"Where are you right now?"

"I'm in the parking lot. About to come back to write my report," Vinh said. "We're still looking for the girl."

"Get back here and come right to my office. We need to discuss a few things."

Before Vinh could respond the call was disconnected.

Groaning, Vinh took out his car keys and wondered how bad the rest of his day was going to be.

CHAPTER EIGHTEEN

"Where are we going?" Sally asked, maybe for the hundredth time.

She kept shuffling along, her feet sliced open and bleeding now, too. She couldn't remember from school how much blood was in a human body. She guessed she'd depleted most of hers by now.

The claws scratching the walls every so often were really irritating her now. She hoped, on the small chance she survived, she'd never hear that sound ever again.

Sally decided to never own a cat or a dog or any pet that had claws. A goldfish would be fine. Nothing that would be able to scrape a nail across a surface and bring her back to this moment in time.

As if you're getting out of here, she thought.

She thought the ground was slowly rising, but that could be that she was delirious and blood loss was playing tricks with her mind. Sally was definitely cold. More than when she'd entered the tunnels to begin with. Wasn't that what happened when you lost a lot of blood? Sally thought she'd had this idea in her head before. Couldn't put it together and remember anymore.

The scraping continued ahead of her.

Sally came around a corner a bit faster since she saw a faint light ahead.

Had she gotten out of Son Doong?

No. She saw there was that strange fungus on the wall that she'd encountered when she first entered the tunnels.

This wasn't where she'd entered, though. This was a different tunnel and it split.

Sally saw the furry creature that had been leading her was standing in the other tunnel, the one without the lichen.

It looked like he raised his arm and pointed at the tunnel past the glowing fungus.

"Go that way? Can you lead me?" Sally asked, doubtful the creature could understand her.

The creature apparently did, because it shook its dark head.

It can't cross the glowing stuff, like it is blocking them. Keeping them inside the tunnels, which is why they've never been seen before, Sally thought.

She took a step into the tunnel but stopped.

"Thank you," Sally said, still hoping this wasn't a trap. Maybe the creature was helping her to get out. Maybe down the tunnel was an exit. Maybe she'd survive after all.

Feeling so weak she didn't know how much longer she could go on, Sally decided not to waste any more time.

The tunnel was definitely rising, which was a good sign to her.

As she started to walk, she glanced back over her shoulder but it was too dark to see if the creature was watching her, or if it had already continued down the tunnel.

She wondered where it would go, and how many more there were. Hoping no one had come looking for her and disturbed them, Sally kept walking.

Up she rose, the tunnel twisting and turning. It wasn't as clean as the ones she'd been in. Even in the dark she could tell it was unused. The ground was bumpy and she was kicking up dust or dirt as she moved. It tickled her nostrils and made her sneeze a few times.

Sally stopped at one point when she thought she heard gunfire, but it was echoing and distant. She hoped none of the creatures had been harmed, and knew she'd be upset if it was her fault.

They should be allowed to live in peace, away from humanity. Left alone so they could be happy.

Sally turned a bend in the tunnel and smiled. She saw a faint beam of light.

Another few meters and she came to another bend, with vines hanging down from the low ceiling. There was a small gap she was able to wiggle through.

And then she was outside again, in the last rays of sunlight.

On a small hill, looking down at a parking lot.

Filled with news vans, police cars, ambulances and military vehicles.

This is all for me, Sally thought and frowned.

She started to walk toward the crowds, hoping she could make it.

I'm not going to tell them about the creature who helped me, so they don't try to look for it and harm it, Sally thought.

Sally got to the parking lot but couldn't go any further. In the light she saw her hand was a mangled mess and there was dried blood all over her legs and hand.

"Help," she tried to yell but nothing came out.

She fell to her knees.

Fighting to not pass out, Sally crawled a few feet before someone noticed her and a woman began to scream for a medic.

Sally closed her eyes. She was going to be fine.

"Sally? It's your papa. Can you open your eyes?"

She didn't know how long she'd been unconscious, but it was likely only a few minutes. She was on a stretcher and being loaded into the back of an ambulance, medics working around her.

"I'm fine. Tired. Hungry," Sally said. She smiled at her parents.

"How did you survive?" It was a police officer standing nearby.

Sally smiled again, thinking of the creature that had shown her the way out. The way back to her family.

"I guess I got lucky and made all the right turns in the tunnels to find the exit," Sally said.

The End

Check out other great

Cryptid Novels!

Ian Faulkner

CRYPTID

Be careful what you look for. You might just find it.1996. A group of 14 students walked into the trackless virgin forests of Graham Island, British Columbia for a three-day hike. They were never seen again. 2019. An American TV crew retrace those students' steps to attempt to solve a 23-year-old mystery.A disparate collection of characters arrives on the island. But all is not as it seems. Two of them carry dark secrets. Terrible knowledge that will mean death for some – but a fighting chance of survival for others. In the hidden depths of the forests – man is on the menu. Some mysteries should remain unsolved...

Eric S. Brown

LOCH NESS HORROR

The Order of the Eternal Light, a secret organization have foretold the end of the human race. In order to save all humanity, agents of the Order must locate the Loch Ness Monster and obtain a sample of its blood for within in it is the key to stopping the apocalypse but finding the monster will be no easy task.

Check out other great

Cryptid Novels!

Edward J. McFadden III

THE CRYPTID CLUB

When cryptozoologist Ash Cohn receives a gold embossed printed invitation inviting him to join The Cryptid Club, he sees the resolution to all his problems.Famous cryptid scientist and biologist, Lester Treemont, one of the world's richest men, and the leader of the Cryptid Club, is dying. What he offers via his invitation is a chance to succeed him. To take over his wealth, laboratory, and discoveries. All Ash has to do is beat eight others like him in a series of tests both mental and physical involving Treemont's collection of cryptids. Seems simple enough, and Ash has nothing to lose.Nine strangers from across the globe, all with reasons for wanting to win. When they start dying one by one, the competition shifts to one of survival. Who among them will rise to the top and reign over The Cryptid Club?

William Meikle

INFESTATION

It was supposed to be a simple mission. A suspected Russian spy boat is in trouble in Canadian waters. Investigate and report are the orders. But when Captain John Banks and his squad arrive, it is to find an empty vessel, and a scene of bloody mayhem. Soon they are in a fight for their lives, for there are things in the icy seas off Baffin Island, scuttling, hungry things with a taste for human flesh. They are swarming. And they are growing. "Scotland's best Horror writer" - Ginger Nuts of Horror "The premier storyteller of our time." - Famous Monsters of Filmland

Check out other great

Cryptid Novels!

Hunter Shea

THE DOVER DEMON

The Dover Demon is real...and it has returned. In 1977, Sam Brogna and his friends came upon a terrifying, alien creature on a deserted country road. What they witnessed was so bizarre, so chilling, they swore their silence. But their lives were changed forever. Decades later, the town of Dover has been hit by a massive blizzard. Sam's son, Nicky, is drawn to search for the infamous cryptid, only to disappear into the bowels of a secret underground lair. The Dover Demon is far deadlier than anyone could have believed. And there are many of them. Can Sam and his reunited friends rescue Nicky and battle a race of creatures so powerful, so sinister, that history itself has been shaped by their secretive presence? "THE DOVER DEMON is Shea's most delightful and insidiously terrifying monster yet." – Shotgun Logic Reviews "An excellent horror novel and a strong standout in the UFO and cryptid subgenres." –Hellnotes "Non-stop action awaits those brave enough to dive into the small town of Dover, and if you're lucky, you won't see the Demon himself!" – The Scary Reviews PRAISE FOR SWAMP MONSTER MASSACRE "B-horror movie fans rejoice, Hunter Shea is here to bring you the ultimate tale of terror!" – Horror Novel Reviews "A nonstop thrill ride! I couldn't put this book down." – Cedar Hollow Horror Reviews

Armand Rosamilia

THE BEAST

The end of summer, 1986. With only a few days left until the new school year, twins Jeremy and Jack Schaffer are on very different paths. Jeremy is the geek, playing Dungeons & Dragons with friends Kathleen and Randy, while Jack is the jock, getting into trouble with his buddies. And then everything changes when neighbor Mister Higgins is killed by a wild animal in his yard. Was it a bear? There's something big lurking in the woods behind their New Jersey home.Will the police be able to solve the murder before more Middletown residents are ripped apart?

www.ingramcontent.com/pod-product-compliance
Lightning Source LLC
Chambersburg PA
CBHW061243170626
46809CB00007B/2806